October Revolution

October Revolution

A NOVEL BY

Tom LaMarr

UNIVERSITY PRESS OF COLORADO

Published by the University Press of Colorado
P.O. Box 849
Niwot, Colorado 80544

The University Press of Colorado is a cooperative publishing
enterprise supported, in part, by Adams State College, Colorado
State University, Fort Lewis College, Mesa State College, Metropoli-
tan State College of Denver, University of Colorado, University of
Northern Colorado, University of Southern Colorado, and Western
State College of Colorado.

Library of Congress Cataloging-in-Publication Data

LaMarr, Tom, 1954–
    October revolution / Tom LaMarr.
            p.   cm.
    ISBN 0-87081-501-6 (alk. paper)
    I. Title.
    PS3562.A4217028   1998
    813'54—dc21   98-26116
                                                         CIP

10   9   8   7   6   5   4   3   2   1

For Anne and my parents, Ruth and LaMar

ACKNOWLEDGMENTS

I am grateful to the following for their assistance: Douglas Unger, Timothy Hillmer, Juliet Wittman, Jane Nunnelee, cousins John Collister and Jadis Norman, brother Bill Jones, Caz Boyd, Rus Caughron, Julie Maddox, Marian Hoffman, Mark Lamprey, and Chet Hampson.

October Revolution

CHAPTER 1

THE FBI IS WATCHING my cats. It's part of the deal we made. Three Denver-based agents were assigned this task, or 1.5 per cat. Fenwick saved me for himself.

We're flying to Washington, D.C., by way of Chicago. Continental Flight 641. "I don't know why they sent me out here," Fenwick is griping. "I'm no baby-sitter, 'specially for the likes of you. I've always thought they should band you guys. You know, those electronic bands they put on birds. We could watch you migrate. Watch you agitate."

Clearly he's not listening to himself. He's dressed like a television evangelist, one of the less successful ones, the ones with tax-free incomes only in the million-dollars-a-year range. His suit is polyester, that shade of blue sold exclusively at Sears. His hair is very short. He hasn't even glanced at the Tom Clancy novel on his lap, open to only the third page.

"So what makes you so goddamned important?" he asks.

"I'm not important," I reply. "I've spent my alleged adult life working at being unimportant."

"You've got a crazy bastard holding hostages in Washington, demanding to see you and no one else. I've been on these assignments for almost thirty years. Back in the sixties, I spied on some of the most famous people you ever heard of, and no one ever took hostages on my account. What the hell was in that book you wrote? What were you? Some sort of hippie communist?"

"That was a long time ago," I remind him. "I was young ... a *weekend* hippie communist. Thankfully, nobody remembers. I'm not important. As you'll recall, he's holding hostages at a Burger King—not the Library of Congress, for Christ's sake."

"Well, somebody remembers."

An orange-haired involuntary spasm of a child squirms to my left, afraid I might again address it. At least it was easy silencing this lamb; timing, as they say, is everything. From the moment the plane accelerated for takeoff, the kid had been reciting a tiresome mantra: "My ears are gonna pop off. My ears are gonna pop off."

I waited with uncharacteristic patience for exactly the right moment—which brought us a message from the pilot: "You can move about the cabin; your ears will not pop off"—to deliver my frantic announcement.

I turned to the kid, leaving only inches between our faces. "My head is exploding!" I screamed. He's been quiet ever since, something I can't say for Fenwick.

"Are you okay?" the Special Agent is asking. "You're not looking too good. Jesus, this can't be your first time on a plane."

"It is, and my curiosity was satisfied before we left the ground. Now I'd just as soon be walking the whole way."

"Getting a little airsick, huh?"

"No, I'm just not used to all these people. I didn't realize an airplane would feel so crowded."

"So you really are some kind of hermit," he says. "I guess our files are right for once. I'm sorry we couldn't charter you your own private jet, but this is taking long enough as it is, with the connection at O'Hare. Your terrorist's going to be asleep by the time we get there. Of course, you'd probably like that. You know, having him disarmed and locked up before your big meeting. Then there'd be no need for courage on your part."

2

"Are you supposed to be talking me out of this? If not, let me remind you I'm here by choice. And I'm still not sure why I agreed to go. Letting this lunatic fall asleep seems perfectly logical to me. I mean, you've got to admit this is all pretty crazy. Terrorists and hostages went out of fashion twenty years ago."

"Well, according to my information, so did you. We couldn't even track down a copy of your book, if you want the hard truth. But that's okay. I know your kind pretty well. That's my job. Has been for almost thirty years. You know, for a lot of us, the sixties were no psychedelic love-in."

I don't remind him that my book was published in 1972, two years post-Love, don't so much as roll my eyes, because I can't let him know I'm still paying attention.

"My problem," Fenwick says, "is I was born too early. I'd like to be about twenty today. Kids these days are too smart for con artists like you. They love this country and they respect their president. Look at Kuwait—they're willing to fight a war at the drop of a hat. No questions asked about who it's for, or how stupid it is. We would have won Vietnam with these kids. Your revolution failed big-time. Look at the war on drugs. We can take your house away if we find a marijuana seed in it. Look at civil rights. The troublemakers are in prison where they belong. Mandatory sentences for 'people of color.' Look at all your tax money going to pay for Star Wars. It doesn't even matter which party is in the White House."

Fenwick closes the novel he's not reading. "All you ever did, Huxley, was find some kids who were even more confused than you were, and then add to their confusion. You didn't think that could be dangerous; you didn't think anyone would get hurt by acting out your half-baked ideas. But you and I know that's not what happened. We know what you started. And my guess is, that's why you're here. You're afraid someone's taking you seriously again, and you know that's a recipe for disaster."

3

There is a moment of silence before Fenwick continues. "Still, you're right about this hostage thing not making any sense. You and your kind, you're history."

Of course, I am as confused as Fenwick is, although he seems to have more experience with that particular condition. I think I know who the terrorist is, but I can't believe he has the edge to take hostages at gunpoint—and I definitely cannot imagine why. Given his family's wealth and the fact that he's known my whereabouts for twenty-five years, he could have conceived a more practical plan for us to finally meet.

I had pulled his letters from my "Success Fallout" file, a tattered Kinney's shoe box, just before I left Denver. My *Cookbook for Revolution: 150 Easy Ways to Boil, Broil, and Fry the Rich* was still selling well when his first letter arrived in early 1973. By that time, the book had brought me $37,463— about $37,463 more than I'd expected to make. On top of that, there was the $582 in small bills the publisher had received in response to my bogus Legal Defense Fund, started by an inventive columnist in the *Village Voice*. My publishers had been kind enough to pass it on to me without taking their usual cut.

But my unexpected windfall paled when I saw the check stapled to the letter from Aaron Hamilton Scott III, Fellow Traveler. Apparently, he was heir to a considerable fortune, and a self-proclaimed revolutionary to boot—what the Marxists would call a useful idiot. The check was for $400,000.

"Hope this keeps you out of jail, brother," he wrote in its lower left corner.

I wanted to return it, telling my father, "No one buys me."

"That simplistic gibberish may sell books these days," he replied, "but we're all for sale, and $400,000 is a lot more than you're worth. You made me your financial advisor; I advise you to keep it. Let me invest it for you. I promise you a guaranteed salary for life of $30,000 per year, no work, no strings, no taxes." (He gave me a cost-of-living raise in 1980, to $45,000. I never asked any questions.)

Now the letters are stashed in my brown grocery bag, my one piece of luggage on this trip. It has "Safeway" printed in big red letters on one side and a large-eared missing child, with whom I now identify, on the other. There's an extra pair of underwear and socks in the bag. A few other essentials. I am traveling light.

I'm sure the FBI would find the letters of interest, especially the most recent one, which arrived several months ago. It was Scott's first missive in seven years, one of only three I'd received in Colorado. "This is it," the brief note warned the world through me. "The Buncombese Liberation Army did not die with the '60s." Oddly enough, the BLA moniker had not appeared until 1974, at least according to my letters. "It's time for action. Time to wake the dead. All power to the BLA."

Scott closed with his equally familiar exit lines: "We will prevail. Death to the $ystem. Peace and Revolution, AHS."

Special Agent Fenwick hasn't noticed that I've carried the bag with me to the lavatory at the rear of the plane. Actually, he doesn't seem to notice much of anything, and I figure I'll use that particular weakness to my advantage. As I shave off my beard with my ancient blue Bic razor, I think back to the chapter I wrote so many years ago, "Throwing a Curve to the Straights." This is the chapter that talks about haircuts, running for state assemblies, marketing home-exercise films. I already know Fenwick has not read it.

I rinse the remnants of my beard down the drain. It makes a strange, even painful sound, a vacuum cleaner run amok, like it's sucking the hair out of the fuselage and into the stratosphere. The face in the mirror is both older and younger than the one I came in with—older in the angles and doughy white-ness of a chin exposed, younger in the pale-brown eyes no longer competing with my graying whiskers. A tiny paper cup delivers enough water to press back my hair. This time, the effect is simply older.

Upon exiting the rest room, I find an unoccupied seat near the back of the plane, along with a newspaper someone has been kind enough to leave for me. This turns out to be the current edition of *USA Today*, a journal as good as any other to hide one's face behind. Its main headline, right next to an article about Brooke Shields, trumpets the now familiar mes-sage "Hostages Held in D.C." I read the article, learning what few details this paper has chosen to share. I am not a criminal, it reminds me, simply a prisoner of circumstance.

It all started late yesterday, when a terrorist in Washington mentioned my name. Wearing an oversized black stocking cap and wielding what one FBI source called a "really big gun," he offered police no clues. All anyone knew was that he wanted to trade his hostages—previously, mild-mannered Burger King customers—for "radical '70s author Rod Huxley." There's a chart at the bottom of the page. Most Americans do not like being held at gunpoint, a survey has revealed.

The landing gear begins its tortured descent. At least, I hope that's what I'm hearing. I look to my left and see a young boy, much smaller than the child who was my first neighbor. But he has those same terrified rabbit-caught-in-the-headlights eyes, and he is moving his lips in silence. I'm no lip reader, but he seems to be shaping the following words: "My ears are going to pop off."

I cup my hands over my ears, just to be safe.

"You need a credit card. Surely you know you can't rent a car with cash."

I pull my hand out of my pants pocket.

"Not even *that* much cash." With cold black beads of eyes, she examines the pile of crumpled twenty-dollar bills, constructing what must be very interesting theories on what so much legal tender is doing in my pocket. Of course, my admission that I'm in a hurry because I need to get away from someone who is getting on my nerves has done little to resolve the problem.

"What I need is a reliable, escort-free mode of transportation," I tell the baroness of Hertz O'Hare. "I need to get to Washington, D.C., and I need to leave now. There's someone there who badly wants to talk with me." I decide to skip the particulars about the hostage situation. "Surely you recognize American currency."

She picks up the handset of her red, dialless phone. "Get me security."

"Have a nice day yourself," I snarl, giving her my yes-you-were-right-I-am-an-escaped-serial-killer look. "Thanks for your valuable time. I'll take my business elsewhere."

Unfortunately, the jerks at Avis are just as bad. They want to know why I don't have a current driver's license. "Come on," I say, "the technology couldn't have changed that much since 1979. I can handle a car." I'm beginning to suspect that Chicago is a gaping black hole—lots of arrivals, no departures—just as it appears on maps of the United States.

At least getting away from Fenwick was easy. As I was leaving the plane, I saw the FBI's Special Agent sandwiched between two stewardesses, stretching tiptoe as he scanned the horizon of hats and hair for my particular crown.

"I'm going to have to ask you to seal off the cabin," he was telling one of the attendants while holding up some kind of ID. "Special Agent Fenwick. FBI. If you give me your cooperation, this will only take a minute."

"Are you sure this is necessary?" she asked. "These pas-

7

sengers have connections to make. We're already running late. I'll have to clear it with my superior."

"Excuse me," I said as I approached, "but if you're looking for a creepy guy with a beard, I think he's hiding in the bathroom."

CHAPTER 2

I FINALLY FIND A CHICAGOAN who takes cash. His politeness, even more than his appearance, suggests he may be an immigrant, too new to the city to know its credit-card-only rules. "Tank you, sir," he says as I turn away, shielding my prize.

The six-dollar hot dog is now in my hands, and I'm squeezing a trail of reluctant pickle slime from a tiny plastic envelope. I am standing at a long, narrow counter—an eating assembly line for businessmen-in-transit who are moving too fast to come to a complete stop—preparing my hot dog. I'm "preparing" it because at six-dollars-plus-tax, it comes naked into O'Hare International, uncloaked even in mustard or ketchup.

Every so often, I see Fenwick between bites. He scurries this way and that, like a crazed city-dwelling squirrel whose tail has just been amputated by the tire of a passing truck. Unsure of which way to turn, he senses he is cornered by traffic. I feel a tinge of sympathy for the beleaguered Special Agent, but I can't imagine listening to him for another three or four hours. Although I do not have a plan for getting into the Burger King without him once I have reached D.C., I am sure I will think of one. At worst, I could call one of Fenwick's superiors—of which there must be many—at the FBI's national office.

Fenwick is still clutching the note I left for him in the plane's tiny bathroom. "I need room to breathe. See you in D.C., provided my cats are okay."

I could have concluded the message, "I'd forgotten how tiring conversation can be, especially the listening part. Thanks for reminding me."

"Let me tell you about the sixties," Fenwick had started in one time, somewhere over Nebraska. "I served as a marine in Vietnam, but I was there too early to see any real fighting. I saw some South Vietnamese soldiers doing the old water torture on a prisoner once. Cong bastard told them everything they wanted to know before they finished him off. It made me think they didn't need our help; they knew what they were doing. That's why I didn't re-up. I know, I know. I was wrong. They really did need our help. The gooks didn't want to fight at all. Most of 'em were in love with old Ho. You know what I think? I think we should have dropped an atom bomb on Hanoi, taught 'em to dick with Uncle Sam."

"It was a colonial war," I interjected with some anger, surprised by the strength of my reaction, "a stupid, inexcusable leftover from the nineteenth century. We should have backed Ho Chi Minh at the end of World War II, and we sure as hell should never have taken over from the French."

"So you're still a communist after all," Fenwick said, smiling slightly. "Now don't get me wrong, I know you're right—well, half right. But what you don't understand is that once we were in, we were in. It was our war, and we should have won it, goddammit. We didn't need a billion Third World midgets laughing behind our backs, and we didn't need our troops returning to ridicule and contempt, to be spit on in the streets."

"I've never met a single veteran who was spat upon, or a protester who admits to using saliva in place of ticker tape," I said. "I'm more inclined to believe that story was concocted by your FBI colleagues in Washington."

"Well, maybe so. Like I said, I didn't re-up. So I guess I shouldn't talk. I never saw any real action. In fact, I didn't get shot at 'til I was back in the States. I'd taken a job as a sort of sheriff's deputy, or maybe I should say deputy's deputy. I was the guy who carried the furniture to the street when they evicted deadbeats in LA's spic neighborhoods. These illegal immigrants would sign $200-a-month leases on their apartments, then think they were in Cuba or Mexico or whatever communist country they came from. They'd buy nice furniture at the Salvation Army, then forget about their rent. I've been shot at by teenage boys, middle-age drunks, eighty-year-old grannies, you name it. But I've only been hit once, and I hit the guy who got me harder. Landed him in the hospital.

"Even so," he continued, "my luck was wearing thin by then. Seems we'd gone into the wrong hovel, and on top of that, I wasn't supposed to be carrying a gun. Damn liberal judge didn't care that this scrote was a squatter, too. Didn't care that old Pedro was a month behind on *his* rent payments, and that I could just as well have been coming for *his* shit-green couch. The county ended up giving him money for his hospital bills and 'psychological trauma.' I got my ass kicked. It got me looking for a better job, I tell you."

He waited for me to react, but I didn't think "Get me the hell out of here—I made a mistake agreeing to this" would help my situation, so I kept that thought to myself.

"What I really wanted was to settle down, get married, have a family," Fenwick told me next. "But I was living in California with all the crazies. All any of the girls wanted was to sit beside swimming pools and smoke drugs. Play tennis in the nude. They wanted Hollywood agents instead of husbands. And, of course, there were people like you stirring things up. That's when I met an FBI recruiter. He told me I could help save America. Told me I could save it from itself."

I looked around for the flight attendant who'd been handing out headphones. Was it too late to change my request?

Fenwick didn't sense my discomfort. He took a sip from his complimentary Diet Coke and said, "The Bureau needed plants—agents who could double as students. So the first thing they did was pay for my college. They sent me to the nuthouse of nuthouses. That's right—Berkeley. Enrolled me as a political science major, then had me join every subversive civil rights group you could name. I met some strange people, I tell you. And I got pretty sick of the smell of marijuana and the sound of the Beatles. So go live in a yellow submarine. Just leave me alone.

"I finally said the wrong thing to one of 'em (a radical, not a Beatle), asked this good-looking broad what a nice girl was doing in the middle of a conspiracy to overthrow the United States government. She turned me in to the top reds, got me thrown out of her group and all the rest of 'em, and then I had to leave the screwball school. Guess she wasn't used to compliments. I did get my degree, though, courtesy of the Agency and someone in the chancellor's office. In recognition of my duty to the university, they said. And I never even finished the first year! But it's a good thing I got it, because the FBI likes its agents to be well educated."

The child to my left was fast asleep, and I was nothing but envious.

"I know what you're thinking," Fenwick said. "I've got a lot to be thankful for. But what really gets my grit is that all I ever wanted was a normal life. And here I am, a bachelor, flying to Buttfuck, Idaho, wherever they need me, on the spur of the moment. And the hippies and revolutionaries? They got good jobs from the banks and law firms they were trying to blow up. Cut their hair and forgot any of it had ever happened. Forgot they'd ever been traitors."

Yet another Chicagoan recognizes American currency. The cab driver demanded forty dollars up front for his troubles, and now he's driving me through a war zone, past the bombed-out shells of once-thriving factories and warehouses with once-thriving parking lots, those outdoor showrooms of industrial muscle, with endless, identical rows of gleaming new 1978 American-made cars, their tires and chrome intact.

"Screw Avis and Hertz and Budget," I say. "A bus trip will give me time to think. Of course, I may find out thinking is the last thing I need."

I see a wary eye in the rearview mirror. "Greyhound's just ahead," the driver grunts. He forgets to add, "Just beyond the gates of hell."

A sign alongside the nearly deserted street says Free Enterprise Zone. But it looks more like a free pickings zone, because the cars I see today have no tires or chrome . . . or windshields or wheels. Finally, across a pockmarked lot, I spy the familiar Greyhound icon. It seems to be leaping to safety. As I get closer, I see I am nearing a refugee camp populated by travelers with barely the means to travel, massed and huddling. We're submerging now, diving to pass beneath a road as empty as this one. And in the dark recess of the underpass there's a shelter of sorts, assembled from cardboard boxes and long-discarded picket signs. "Greyhound Unfair to Labor." "Greyhound: Leave the Conniving to Us."

The message on these signs is still valid, of course, even this many years after the actual picketers were connived out of their jobs. And I'm reminded that the workers most qualified to drive sixteen-ton buses are now serving burritos at Taco Bell, alongside the real air traffic controllers. I shouldn't patronize this company. But I've already soiled myself by flying Continental, and I can think of no other way to get to Washington, apart from hitchhiking. And that's about as appealing to me today as appearing on television talk shows to sensationalize my days as a radical author, something I've been asked to do two or three times. At least I can take comfort in knowing that the drivers and mechanics to whom I'm entrusting my life are not getting fat and lazy on their minimum wages.

Still, the driver seems offended when I ask, "Have you ever driven one of these things before?"

His answer, "Once or twice," is delivered without any hint of sarcasm.

I find a seat over the back wheels and dig in its crack for a nonexistent seat belt.

"Don't worry, Jesus will protect you," the pimple-ridden teenager across the narrow aisle assures me.

"I thought the driver looked familiar," I say, reaching into my Safeway bag for a letter, any letter, which I will duly pretend to read. Trying to look occupied. I wonder if they still call themselves Jesus Freaks but know better than to initiate an interminable one-sided conversation by asking. After all, if that's what I wanted, I would have stayed with Fenwick.

The cratered apostle returns to his Bible study, flipping through well-worn, red-trimmed pages, searching for a rebuttal to his own triviality. For the first time, I notice the Greyhound's smell. It's something akin to rotting apples and cigarette butts, the smell of too many people sitting for too long in one place. But at least the bus has an odor, unlike the airplane and airport, their life signs sterilized beyond human recognition. I hear more passengers climbing aboard. The bus is still idling.

I make the mistake of looking up and don't like what I see. Two massive blocks of drab, official blue are coming toward me, staring at me, coming for me. They walk with deliberate slowness, concentrating less on speed and more on the intensity of the hatred in their cold, colorless eyes. Their footsteps aren't heavy, but the goose-step precision of their quiet march provides the only sound in this void. Its volume is deafening.

This is my first look at real-life Chicago cops. Like every-one else who was alive in 1968, I have seen their television work—that prime-time "police riot" of blurred clubs and bleeding faces, the day-after photographs of battered hippies and journalists. Where are the network cameras now that it's my turn? I know I am going to die—or come as close to it as possible without actually attending a coroner's inquest—before my broken body is returned to Fenwick. And it won't even make CNN.

Ironically, I remember addressing this situation in "Throw-ing a Curve to the Straights." "When cornered by thugs wearing badges, and there are no television cameras as your witness," I advised my readers, "submit to injustice." Be agree-able, even polite. "If they press you for the identities of co-conspirators and fellow travelers, give them the names of upstanding citizens, of bankers and the like, school board mem-bers, and reactionary professors. Offer up your parents in sacrifice. However, if there is a camera present, the rules are changed. Fight the Power with all your passion and might. Kick at the belly of the pig oppressor as he drags you to the paddy wagon."

Now they are only a few feet away from me—close enough for me to read the "We Serve and Protect" on their badges. In unison they stop, stare for another minute or two, then lunge at a small black man with big gold chains who just happens to be sitting directly in front of me. I can't see much of him apart from the back of his head and the jewelry hanging like Christmas tree garlands from his neck. His hair is oily and straight—what Malcolm X would have called a "self-defacing conk"—and he's wearing a pair of narrow Ray Charles sunglasses.

"Let's see that bag," the larger of the two public servants barks.

"Hey, man, what's the hassle? I ain't got nothing to hide."

15

They interpret this as the man's consent to search his belongings, which they undertake with the vigor and dedication to duty I remember from the 1968 Convention reports. His few items of spare clothing are tossed from a dry-cleaning bag like so many limp, forehead-flattened yippies. An extra pair of narrow snakeskin shoes bounces on the grooved rubber mat.

"Yo, man, you ain't got no right."

"No, *you* ain't got no rights," the smaller cop replies. "We got your permission to search this bag . . . and search you, inside and out, if we have to. Wait a minute. Hold everything. Looks like we got something here."

He lifts a two-inch joint from the bag with a delicateness I have not previously seen displayed and slowly raises it to the round ceiling lamp as if he has recovered the Holy Grail.

"Bingo," he says.

"Aw, man. I've got fifteen hours to sit on this bus," the victim pleads. "I brought that along so I wouldn't be gettin' no carsickness."

"You won't have to worry 'bout that now," Big Cop says. "Stand up and put your hands in these." The cuffs provide a convenient handle for dragging the man at a 45-degree angle up the aisle and down the steps, plunkety plunkety plunk. No one says a word. It is the silence of fear, of please don't come for me next.

After a wait of about twenty minutes, the bus finally starts, two-thirds empty. There's no one in the seat next to mine. Just Fenwick, asking the same stupid, brilliant, piercing questions. The ones I couldn't face hearing.

"So did you really think you'd never have to pay the price for your half-assed hippie games? Did you really think there were hiding places in this world?"

He's not really here, of course, on Greyhound 665 to Pittsburgh-Baltimore-Washington. But his questions are real enough.

CHAPTER 3

YESTERDAY, I WAS OUT FOR one of my free-form walks, meaning I could wind up anywhere. It was a perfect fall day, the sun a bright patch of haze in the afternoon smog. The wind brushed leaves into brilliant swirls of color and light, the ghosts of French Impressionists at work, while squirrels bombarded hapless pedestrians with stinging acorns.

Like everyone else in the world—with one now important exception—I was not thinking about the "revolutionary sixties," or that slim, sophomoric volume with my name on the cover. I was simply walking. Deliberately lost.

At the intersection of Colfax and Pearl, she approached from my right. She was singing a gospel song, steel-throated strong, Alabama summer hot. The song was new to me. "My momma told me, you sinners can't hide. My momma told me, you sinners can't hide." Then she was only a few feet from me, a night-black woman, simple red dress draped loosely over her long, dark limbs, her hair pulled back in braids, taut, like the skin on her face.

When she saw me, she did not close her mouth and lower her head, pretending nothing had happened, as I would have done. "My mother and father told me a sinner can't hide," she told me instead, and resumed her musical testimony.

I nodded my head in polite agreement and hurried back to my three-room apartment on Corona Street. This was the place where I did most of my hiding.

For twenty years, I had been able to sneak in and out of the real world. I was one of America's invisibles, privately mapping a city's grid of sidewalks and alleys, sitting alone in movie theaters, or at home, between the lopsided towers of half-read paperbacks that form artificial walls in my imitation–New York–in–the–1930s art-deco apartment, drinking my bourbon and Coke, masturbating to impersonal fantasies, taunting the cats with dancing string. Looking for God, a reason to continue, an excuse to stop.

For twenty years, I sought anonymity beneath the brown cloud of pollution that shields Denver from harmful sunlight. In three rooms with one meager window—barred with steel and framing the gold-plated dome of the Colorado state capitol—I was mostly content, though I had known plenty of long, boring days that limped along like dogs clipped by cars, begging to be put out of their misery.

Today, I remember them all as blissful.

Today began abruptly with the early morning wake-up call from my father.

"They're holding sausages for you at a Burger King restaurant in Washington, D.C.," I thought he said.

I told him I wasn't ready to eat yet, that sleep sounded much more appealing. But I was flattered to be the one he'd chosen to call to share the first signs of the impending breakdown of his logical-to-a-fault mind. Maybe he was regressing to our first years together, when I was still his child and subordinate and he was omniscient and powerful—an arrangement he missed in later years.

"I said there are terrorists holding hostages and they're demanding to see you," he repeated.

Now I was questioning my own mental agility. "Why would anyone . . ."

"It makes no sense to me, either," he said. "I strongly suggest you turn on your television and see if they offer any clues. It looks as if you may be in for a very interesting day."

The world had changed, as suddenly and inexplicably as it always did. And it was not just my world. Against years of planning and precaution, I was a pebble sending ripples into the vast, unfeeling ocean. However I chose to respond to this news, whether by hiding in my apartment or answering the terrorists' demand, I would impact the lives of others.

As I absorbed the dreary glow of *Good Morning America* and saw my younger, less innocent face—framed by fur, eyes ablaze—I remembered the letter I'd received a few months before, the announcement that Aaron Hamilton Scott had returned to life.

This is it indeed. Time to wake the dead.

"What could they possibly want?" I asked my father. "Do you think my life is in danger?"

"It is clearly in danger of changing," he replied. "You'll probably have to go there, you realize. You can't spend the *next* twenty years wishing you had done something to help avert catastrophe."

The chirpy hosts of *Good Morning America* switched topics as often as they ran commercials. Get a head start on your spring lawn care. Foolproof tips on outrunning inflation, tested on actual fools. Just as they were bringing out the latest necrophiliac-disguised-as-a-biographer ("Coming up, an author who claims the late Jim Henson was a cross dresser who abused his puppets") and just after I finally got my first look at Joel somebody, the movie critic who's always quoted in newspaper ads because he never dislikes anything, I was jolted by a rapping on my door. Five simple beats, evenly measured. My thoughts scattered like roaches at the first flash of light.

"Are you Roderick Thurgood Huxley, author of *Cookbook for Revolution*?" the tall but chunky man in the hallway inquired. When I gave him the answer he was anticipating, he flashed his blindingly silver badge before my eyes.

"FBI. Special Agent Fenwick. Can I come in?"

I was both angered and flattered to learn the extent of the information the FBI maintained on me. "So what else do you have in my file?" I asked Fenwick.

"Only that you're lazy," he replied.

"It says I'm lazy?"

"Not in so many words, perhaps. But that is the reason you dropped out of the public eye, isn't it? That and the bee thing."

"I stopped for ideological reasons," I contended. "My book was being misinterpreted. It was causing harm. I'd seen this firsthand."

"That's the response I expected. I studied up on you on the flight here," Fenwick said. "But I don't know. After reading your file, I'm amazed you were able to produce an entire book of any kind, let alone one that would cause such commotion. What was it the lefties called it?" He was referring to the reviewer for *Ramparts* magazine. "'The only book that matters'? You sure don't strike me as the most motivated person I've ever met. How did it happen?"

I was on fire; that's the only way I can describe it. For years, my mind smoldered and sputtered, burning myself and those around me with strange, uncontrollable ideas. In high school, I was suspended time after time for mimeographing smart-ass "underground newspapers" after hours in the teachers' lounge, for organizing skip days, for being trapped in a small-town Midwestern high school while the late 1960s raged.

My hastily scribbled essays, fresh from the study hall just ended, were the first things read each afternoon in Mrs. Moscone's English class. My teachers (some of them) thought I was a gifted eccentric. "Yours is one name I expect to see again," Mr. Burdon, the yearbook editor, told me, although one industrial arts instructor tried to remove that possibility by removing me from the Class of '68. "I'll give a hundred bucks to anyone who shoots that wise-ass commie bastard," one of my shop-inclined friends quoted Mr. Parker as saying. "I'm serious." It was, to my knowledge, the single highest bounty ever offered for a student of Dubuque High.

When school let out, I wandered the sidewalks of The Hill, past Sandy's Drive-In and the Westminster Church lawn, where weekend hippies with stringy hair and cutoff shorts passed joints back and forth and griped about "the pigs." Cars roared past with radios blaring; Frisbees caught the glint of a late-day sun. "Are you a boy or a girl?" passersby would shout, or, "Get a haircut, faggot," and we knew we were better than our surroundings.

"Drugs and riots," my father ranted when I told him of my plans to attend school in Iowa City and pick up the fame being held for me in the University of Iowa Fiction Writers' Workshop. "Your tuition here is paid for; it's one of the few benefits of my position. You will be attending school here." When I threatened to terminate my education altogether, he said, "They're not awarding many student deferments to hippies or janitors." And so I enrolled at Dubuque Catholic College, where my father taught business and accounting on automatic pilot or sat in a cramped cubicle with his name on the door—it should have read, "*Beware of* Professor Benton Huxley"—reviewing scholarly journals that did not mention his name, jealously watching advances in thought—and accounting—from the sidelines of academia.

Ironically, my father had spent much of his adult life hoping to transfer away from DCC. He wanted to be "on the playing field," as they say, where generous state funds paid for bigger offices and more sophisticated computers, nearer the myth of Progress he worshiped. But those more prestigious posts required publication, and my father was too lazy to commit his thoughts, such as they were, to paper. DCC had no such requirements.

Unfortunately for my father, one Huxley did succeed in getting published while at DCC. Worse yet, the essay I composed for the student paper was adopted by the school's self-proclaimed intelligentsia. Within weeks, I was Dubuque's leading exponent of revolutionary thought. I saw my "Recipe for Revolution" stapled to telephone poles along College Boulevard, even heard it quoted by one of my father's peers.

"'The war goes on, here and in Southeast Asia,'" DCC's resident English guru, Elmore Stinchcomb, parroted before the seven mostly full chairs in his afternoon literature class. "'But we have a recipe for victorious revolution. Take ten million angry students. Add a dash of racism and genocide. Blend thesis with antithesis and bring to a boil. The government of Richard Daley and Lyndon Johnson and Richard Nixon has declared war on the people. Corruption and conquest. Napalm and lies. The people must now fight back, take the streets, then take the day. We need new leaders and laws. So point that flag at somebody else. Legalize dope. Legalize love. Legalize intelligent thought.'"

"Right on, Rod," Stinchcomb exclaimed upon finishing the manifesto, stroking his auburn goatee with long, thin fingers.

"Recipe for Revolution" brought an unexpected bonus by nearly stopping my father's heartbeat. "This is *my* town. *My* school. You're supposed to be *my* son; couldn't you at least act the part?"

I completed a second essay entitled "Parents, Politicians, and Other Trained Liars." It, too, appeared in the student paper, alongside a College Republicans ad warning the silent but watchful majority of a "new barbarian invasion." The pairing seemed only appropriate, as the photo used to illustrate this threat could well have been mine, from the fuzzy failure of a beard to the stoned but angry eyes.

"Is this your way of showing us how superior you are?" my father queried, exhibiting a surprising depth of insight. "Is it that you have become too big for your family? Or Dubuque, perhaps?"

"I'm sorry if I'm embarrassing you, Father. But I'm doing the one thing I can in small-town Du-puke to stop Nixon and his unholy war. In case you haven't noticed, there's a new world coming. Centuries of bigotry and fear are being swept away, and I want to have my hand on the broom handle." Incredibly, except for the part about not wanting to embarrass my father, I had never been more sincere.

It was late in my junior year that I saw the rest-room graffiti that changed my life. On the side of the metal stall, someone had scratched a cold silver message into the dark brown paint: "DCC diplomas. Free. Take one." An arrow pointed to the toilet paper dispenser. Three days later, I told my father I was again thinking of applying to the University of Iowa.

"There's absolutely nothing wrong with DCC," I said. "If you want to be a nun, that is." This was true, as the school had only recently gone coed in order to attract increased financing, and its most successful graduates were indeed nuns and church administrators.

"Always the smart aleck," he countered. "Although you may not have noticed, the nuns make excellent students. You, on the other hand, don't seem inclined to make anything out of yourself."

"They have no other diversions apart from your accounting assignments," I said. "I'm going to a real school." This time, he was glad to know I was leaving Dubuque.

Fifteen students sat around the circular table in Room 436, English-Philosophy Building, home to the venerable

University of Iowa Fiction Writers' Workshop. Each week, two mimeographed pieces of writing were submitted for classwide critique. I'd pick them up in the workshop office half an hour before class, skim them, and scribble a pair of good reviews. Others took the process more seriously, and I was always amazed by the amount of time that went into each one-paragraph condemnation.

"This story shows a mastery of depicting unmotivated hatred and unexplained behavior," one read. "The television soap operas are crying out for your gift."

Another, "Don't drop your accounting courses."

It was the same each week. After an offending would-be writer heard the charges read aloud by the workshop head, he would squirm quietly, waiting for class to end. Then he would invariably invoke the Tennessee Williams defense, telling any sympathizers within earshot as they darted for the stairs, "He got a C for *Glass Menagerie,* you know."

I was in the undergraduate section, although nearly all of the students were twenty-five, thirty, even older. They'd been to dozens of schools, millions of places—Europe, Vietnam, the fucking moon. Apart from the Gang of Four—a cluster of older students who sat together with identical stone-faced expressions, looking as if they were posing for a critics' Mount Rushmore—I mainly remember the students who were near my age. There were Matt and Pete, good people and convincing storytellers. L.R.E. Flanders, the bespectacled science fiction writer. "Do you think you have enough initials?" one of his critics had asked him on paper. And Sara Lynn Caine. She became my biggest supporter, among other things.

Of course, I couldn't forget Ernest Gripp, the workshop director. He must have been sick the day my writing samples were approved by the admissions board. He certainly made it clear that he considered me out of my depth when my mimeographed piece was discussed by the class. It concerned a stockbroker named Harrold Von Eaton who'd been abducted by and replaced by his garbage. Mrs. Von Eaton solved the mystery only after he had left for work, recalling that there had been an unusual number of flies circling about her husband at breakfast.

Months earlier, Stinchcomb had praised my invention, telling me it was fit for publication. Gripp disagreed—emphatically. "Even though your friends seem to approve," he sneered, noting correctly that the piece had been one of the few to receive a positive reaction from a majority of my classmates, while at the same time implying I had deviously purchased their loyalty, "I am far from impressed. This is not a story. It's a joke. And as a joke, I presume it is supposed to be funny. And again, some of your friends seem to think it is just that. I have no problem with unrealized attempts at humor. As far as I see it, there is really only one problem with this piece, Mr. Huxley. You do not know how to write."

Gripp spoke these words with incontestable authority, with a deep, almost booming voice, a secular Moses intimidating his fellow tribesmen. It was a manner he affected with consistency, as if he were constantly rehearsing for a reading of his own work before an audience of hundreds, none of whom could hear very well.

"This is what results when a skilled typist lacks the patience to edit and revise," he elaborated for the benefit of the class, "and to ultimately bring the reader into his story. It took me four minutes to read it. I suspect it took Mr. Huxley about that long to write it, maybe a few more to retype it."

I understood his point; hell, he'd summed me up with cruel precision. But he could never understand that writing for five minutes was a torturous undertaking if you possessed only a four-minute attention span—or worse, if your mind was smoldering, constantly threatening to burst into flame. Thinking about it now, I'm sure he saw me as a cliché of sorts, a smart-assed, semi-educated "new barbarian" hiding behind the shallow sincerity of youth, behind long hair and standard-issue student uniform, too goddamned lazy to read the millions of words that made up Western literature, too lazy even to edit the two or three hundred of his own. I think he believed the same thing about everyone in the 1971–1972 undergraduate workshop.

The Gang of Four agreed with Gripp's assessment, if not with his reasoning. "Like another, more famous Huxley, our Rod wants to escape from this world, thereby trivializing it. What we have here is another brazen example of the decadent, reactionary, running-dog-lackey bourgeois corruption of Marxist dialectic that is threatening everywhere to undermine our great socialist struggle." Their anonymous spokesman concluded by instructing me to burn it.

But as Gripp conceded, my friends outnumbered them.

"I just read the story again. God, this is really wacky and curious. I love to laugh. Your story makes me laugh." Gripp didn't have to read the student's name for me to know that Sara had liked "The Harrold Von Eaton Affair."

I called her the Breeze because she came up suddenly, silently, as if from nowhere. She was the kind of person an aunt would call sweet—quiet yet friendly. She called me an artist, said I was meant to change people's thinking, to "burn everyone who stands in your path with your scorched-earth approach to writing."

This all sounded good to me at the time, and I badly wanted to believe that Sara was blessed with some superhuman insight. But even then, with my twenty-one-year-old ego pushing for that theory, I knew there was a more plausible explanation. My classmate had a crush on me.

Sara was not unattractive, but she was not especially attractive either. She was a little thin in places, and her short, dark hair did not help soften the boyishness of her face. Neither did the wisp of down on her upper lip.

What Sara did have was a very expressive face. When she was cheerful, which was most of the time, her pale blue eyes sparkled like sunlight on shallow water. When she was enthused, which was nearly as often, her passion could be infectious.

She breezed into me once at an antiwar march—the last of the fall semester. "Rod, hi. I see I'm not the only one bored with studying for finals. Did I tell you how much I liked your story? I'm really looking forward to seeing the next one." With the help of 300 other students huddled at the base of Hillcrest Dormitory, which towered some eight stories above us, we closed down Highway 6. We even made the front page of Dubuque's *Telegraph Herald*—another gift for my father. Garbage cans filled to the rim with water crashed to the pavement, heaved from the roof of Hillcrest, exploding like mines near the police line.

When shortsighted cops retaliated by shooting tear gas canisters into the dorm, we were joined by hundreds of reinforcements, and soon, our march for peace was preempted by a straight-off-the-six-o'clock-news riot. "This is getting dangerous," I said, and Sara agreed it was time to disappear. We had a couple of Whoppers at Iowa City's new Burger King, one of the first buildings to appear on the pedestrian mall, flagship to a fleet of urban renewal projects.

"I've got to confess to proletarian tastes in food," I told her. "I love these goddamned things." An hour later I was in Sara's two-room place on North Summit Street, pinned to her mattress on the hardwood floor. Again, her passion was infectious.

That night, in an apartment on a hill in a landlocked Midwestern state, I felt the ocean. Buoyed by gentle waves, our rhythms interlocking, Sara and I were willingly carried, respectful of the tide, of its great primeval force. We were rocked and massaged, made to feel weightless, all while I savored the taste of her salt. When the waters turned violent—heaving us starward then letting us fall, and causing us to cling together more fiercely—we found passion in the danger. And when the tide finally released us from its pull, we were emptied, unable to move. Like jellyfish beached on the sand. Invertebrated.

"That was fantastic," I whispered while stroking her hair and experiencing each breath as if it was something new. "You were fantastic."

Sara blushed, and I thought she was beautiful.

Late the next morning, she readied two bowls of Cheerios. And she made me smile by saying, "We'll have to do this again sometime."

"Tonight would be good," I told her.

It was Sara who first read my "Recipe for Revolution" essays and convinced me I should take them to the *Burning Fist,* Iowa City's premier revolutionary freebie. The idea took hold of me, for all the obvious reasons. In less than two semesters, the workshop had taught me only to distrust my instincts about writing fiction. One person's "excess verbiage" was another's "economical prose." It was all too confusing, too subjective. It was . . . hard work. And Sara had reminded me of an easier approach.

The *Fist* printed portions of my manifesto.

"This really is the start of a new age," the red-haired, rattle-nerved editor, Rad Brad, confided to me at our first meeting, "and we're gonna usher it in. No more greed or hypocrisy. No war heroes, Shriners, or priests, brother. This is the end of history as we know it."

Beneath his thick glasses, two narrow slits blinked constantly, as if responding to some invisible stimuli—to bright suns or thick clouds of smoke that no one else could see. His father, I learned, had been a journalist in Chicago, and Rad had come to Iowa City for the same reason I had—to be officially certified as a writer. I learned, too, that his writing samples had not been accepted by the workshop admissions board.

One afternoon in late April, when I was walking to my last workshop session, I saw a disheveled, drunken student— like my secret self, hardly a revolutionary purist—distributing the *Fist* in front of the English-Philosophy Building. I saw Mr. Gripp approaching, then getting a copy shoved in his face. Angrily, Gripp snatched the paper, tucking it under his arm as he pushed open the glass doors.

"I didn't realize we had a published author in our midst," he confessed during the class I should have skipped. "I didn't realize Mr. Huxley was the political type, but this, certainly, is political type."

His opinion didn't matter. The *Fist* kept getting demands for more copies. I was asked to deliver the eulogy at a mock funeral for Richard Nixon. Screw Ernest Gripp and my father. I could write. I got an idea: I would send my manifesto to the big publishers in New York, along with a note from Rad, telling them about the incredible demand for this watershed work.

"No, I've got a better idea," Rad replied when I asked him for the reference. "I'll publish it. We can raise some spare change, print 500 copies or so. If those sell, tomorrow the world, brother."

Sell they did, and by the middle of July, Rad was talking about a second expanded printing. Rad and I got stoned and walked all over the campus, pretending we had no necks and that our heads were hovering independently above our bodies, remotely controlled through some sort of telepathy. The bright lights and neat rows of buildings looked as if they were part of a model electric train set. We sat at the edge of dark fields and looked down at the stars, Rad reminding me that there's no such thing as "up" in space.

"Don't fall off the Earth," he'd caution.

We talked about climbing into his '57 Rambler station wagon and heading west to California to see the country we were overthrowing. We'd locate Carolyn Cassady, widow of Neal, maybe crash the Republican Convention in San Diego. Rumor had it that Lennon and Dylan would be there, "singing for the people." Like many good pipe dreams, it swelled into a fragrant cloud, growing increasingly complex and ambitious, then faded into the air like so much hash and marijuana smoke.

Unknown to Rad—and over Sara's objections—I had pursued my initial plan. Five New York publishers had received my letters, along with an accounting of the book's local success.

When I heard from Meiser & Grubb, I didn't have the nerve to call my friend and comrade to share the news. In fact, I would not face him again while I remained in Iowa City, although to my embarrassment, he would try speaking with me.

Meiser gave Rad $500 for his "rights." I never doubted it was to keep him from sabotaging the project.

The ultimate title, *Cookbook for Revolution: 150 Easy Ways to Boil, Broil, and Bake the Rich,* belonged to my editor, Clifford Moss. And it had taken him hours of argument to convince me that my proposed title, *Roasting the Pigs (And Eating the Leftovers),* was even more of a cliché and had probably been used as the title of "other amateurish endeavors more suited for mimeograph reproduction."

Moss also contributed much of the book's humor, both the intended and accidental entries. "You're doing all the work,"

I complained early into the project. "I thought you wanted a writer, not someone to star in your book."

"If we wanted a writer," Moss corrected me with typical candor and coldness, "we would have found one." I felt as if I had answered a want ad in the Iowa City *Press Citizen* for "Revolutionary figurehead. Send name only. Actual physical presence not required."

As each evening blurred into night, Moss pecked frantically at his Selectric typewriter as if he were the last surviving crew member on a sinking ship, futilely signaling for help in Morse code. "We've got a hot book here," he said during a rare break, "provided we can get it out before the fad dries up. This could make my career—and make you a few bucks, of course." The silver-dollar-sized bald spot on the back of his head, surrounded appropriately by light brown, mosslike hair, gleamed beneath the solitary desk lamp. Two tiny, neatly stacked manuscripts were reflected in his wire-rimmed glasses, completely concealing his eyes.

"He's crazy," I told Sara the one time I phoned her from my room at the Edison Hotel in New York's theater district.

"*He's* crazy? How can you go behind your best friend's back like this? You know Brad was determined to help you publish your book. And after he's done so much for you."

"This is bigger than Rad Brad," I contended, "bigger than any of us. He has to know he can't do *Cookbook* justice."

"Well, you should talk with Brad when you come back," Sara suggested. "He's pretty upset. And he's not alone. You are coming back, aren't you?"

"Of course I am, but I'm not sure when. Moss has me manacled to a desk in his office. I was up 'til two o'clock last night, arguing with him on every detail. I've hardly been in my room here at the hotel, and I haven't seen any of New York, unless you count staring at prostitutes from the back of a cab. This is turning out to be a lot more work than it's worth.

"And," I added, "something even more distasteful is taking place. As I was saying, I fight Moss, point for point, but it makes no difference. My *Cookbook* is turning into his book, even if my name will be the one on the cover. I'm tempted to turn and run, away from all this greed and shortsighted hypocrisy."

"Then why don't you?"

"I'm not sure. I really am not sure." I couldn't tell her it was because I was salivating like one of Pavlov's pups at the thought of seeing my name on that cover. "I guess I'm here because the message is too important to be limited to lots of 500 copies," I said, trying to persuade myself as well. "Even if it is being diluted, the truth is getting out. And they are taking my *Cookbook* seriously. Moss says it'll go straight to typesetting the second we're through with it. He wants to see it in bookstores by the end of the year. Everyone here is completely behind it." I didn't bother to repeat Moss's other comment: "A typo here and there won't matter in a book like this."

A few days before I set out hitching to New York, Sara and I attended a Friends of Old-Time Music concert in Hatcher Auditorium. There, four very old black men who could barely walk to their wooden folding chairs strummed acoustic guitars and sang dozens of classic blues songs they had composed decades earlier, songs with titles like "Nobody Knows You When You're Down and Out" and "Key to the Highway," all of which, I was sure, were credited to "public domain" on my Eric Clapton and Rolling Stones albums.

"This is as close to heaven as we may ever get," Sara beamed, and I actually shared her enthusiasm. I think it was, for both of us, a combination of good hash, sexual anticipation, and hopefulness about my book—in Sara's words, its importance to the world. The genius of the performers had something to do with it, too.

"They didn't have shows like this in Storm Lake," she said, reminding me that much of her passion—for everything—was the result of growing up in a town the size of my graduating class. To Sara Caine, Iowa City was a metropolis, as were Des Moines and Cedar Rapids. Now, sitting on the narrow bed in my Manhattan hotel room, I wanted her with me. "I'll call you as soon as I get back," I told her over the phone. "I promise."

Moss continued to write his book, unobstructed by my presence. "Conning the Establishment" became "Throwing a Curve to the Straights." "Parents, Politicians, and Other Liars" became "Over Thirty, Underhanded"—two things Moss seemed to know very well.

But the changes were only beginning. Within months of *Cookbook*'s publication, the FBI national office requested a copy of my growing file from the regional Iowa office. A frog-faced, cigar-sucking politician in North Carolina publicly demanded I be tried for treason. Moss got his promotion. And me, I became *Time* magazine's "young revolutionary to watch."

CHAPTER 4

"WASHINGTON, D.C., A CAPITAL CITY," the sign announces, just as our driver aims his bus for the deepest pothole on New York Avenue and the Bible scholar falls back into silent prayer, his eyes tightly closed.

The ride has been a long one. There was a swerve in Pennsylvania, more of a jerk really, making me wonder if the driver had fallen asleep for a few seconds—and keeping me awake the rest of the trip.

Not that I minded completing this trek with my eyes propped open, given the nightmares I had each time I closed them. "So who's in that Burger King?" Fenwick asked me in one. He was standing next to Ernest Gripp. "Aaron Hamilton Scott III? Or maybe Rad Brad? This wouldn't be a publicity stunt for another book, would it? God knows you'd need something big."

Worse still were the dreams about bees.

To my surprise, I discover there's a Burger King attached to the bus station, but it isn't the famous one. I stop for a midmorning Whopper and fries and observe bus station business as usual: the mingling of near penniless travelers with their potential muggers. I pick up the scattered remains of a *Washington Post* and locate the front page. But the headline I am looking for—"Terrorist Falls Asleep"—isn't there. Neither is the appropriate text: "Aaron Hamilton Scott III, heir to the Scott rubber band fortune, was apprehended late last night without violence. He currently resides in an FBI cell, patiently waiting to meet with onetime radical author Rod Huxley and discuss bygone times."

The actual headline reads, "Beirut on the Potomac," and the front section is devoted almost entirely to that geographic disparity. I scan its contents to see if Scott has revealed his intentions for me. Perhaps we are to host a joint news conference announcing the establishment of a provisional Buncombese Liberation Army Amerikan People's Government. Or perhaps he simply plans to keep me as a rich person's pet, having come to Washington to collect his purchase from all those years ago, his personal Thomas Paine, something to parade at cocktail parties when it's not chained in the basement of Daddy's mansion, dutifully producing pamphlets for the Underground.

But an article entitled "Who's Holding the Burger King?" reminds me the mystery is mine to solve. Even more surprisingly, my escape from the FBI has failed to impress the *Post*'s jaded senior editors. Their paper contains no new information on my predicament whatsoever, and all I learn is that the FBI, "in the interest of Huxley's safety," is refusing to meet with the press, even while Washington's police chief is publicly asking, on only the second morning of the siege, "Why is it taking the Bureau so long to deliver Huxley? That terrorist has got to be losing patience. If they don't do something soon, we'll be seeing Burger King patrons in body bags, I'm certain."

As little as I know about my terrorist, *I* am certain he won't start dropping his guests to simply relieve the boredom of waiting. If anything, the chief's words only renew my determination to somehow find another way to Scott, one that does not require an FBI delivery.

There is a scuffle in the corridor that leads to the rest rooms. "Take your shit and get out of here," a woman is shouting. I return my attention to the last of my fries, along with an editorial that's considerably more difficult to swallow. It is entitled "Our Back Pages."

"We baby boomers are a narcissistic, self-glorifying lot, blindly in love with our common past, many of us living in that past," columnist Mona Epcott moans.

> Now it is time for us all, not just Rod Huxley, to realize that actions have consequences, that stupid words beget stupid deeds. It is time an entire generation put itself on trial. Time we stopped allowing the hazy glow of nostalgia to obscure our devastating mistakes: songs that advocated the rejection of authority and the abuse of logic-retarding drugs; alleged antiwar leaders who instigated a different kind of war, bringing its violence to the college campus; the 'If it feels good, do it' ethic that led to AIDS, fatherless families, and national bankruptcy, both economic and moral. We were the generation that was going to save the world, then wallow forever in it, eternally young, as if we had not already enjoyed an overly pampered, overly protracted childhood. In retrospect, all we had was our youth and its attendant arrogance. The youth is long gone. It is time now for the arrogance to follow.

By the time I finish, I'm feeling almost nostalgic. I think of the ideas and ideals that have not stopped making sense, even if we have stopped living them. I think of a certain imperialistic war that our different kind of war brought to an end. What was it Bob Dylan sang in the composition that inspired the editorial's title? "Ah, but I was so much older then, I'm younger than that now." Mona would never understand it.

Whatever time it is according to the *Post,* the clock in the Burger King—next to the "No sitting in booths for more than fifteen minutes" sign—tells me it's time to go. It is almost ten-thirty. After consulting my "So This Is Your First

Visit to Washington" map, I head north on Twelfth, looking for a K Street.

Living in Colorado, I had forgotten about humidity, but the Washington air reminds me with every movement and breath. Compared with my dehydrated Denver, its atmosphere a light bouquet of carbon monoxide, sulphur, and mile-high oxygen, this to me is like walking underwater, my body weighed down by the invisible mass. Still, K arrives earlier than I expected, and as I journey west on its wide, bustling sidewalk, I notice that the buildings are becoming taller. I am entering the downtown.

Already, I can see the massive barricade—the writhing, human wall—about four blocks ahead. At this distance, the strange, thousand-legged creature looks like a phosphorescent centipede, bathed as it is in the eerie, multicolored glow of flashing emergency lights. The scene has all the makings of a cheap Japanese monster movie, circa 1960, especially when I imagine that the nonmoving automobiles and trucks to my right have been abandoned, their terrified owners fleeing to a false promise of safety.

Needless to say, however, the drivers are still locked firmly in place by their seat belts, and pedestrians are moving all around me, seemingly unaffected by the commotion, like the ones I see sauntering into the Know Your Oats health food store. They could be the same customers I've seen outside similar stores in Denver, miracle seekers in their thirties and forties, suffering from cheeseburger deprivation, their religious-like devotion in harsh contrast to their pale, puffy faces and troubled-teen complexions.

Walking past a park, if that's what contemporary city planners call a paved-over block with a few well-placed trees and benches, I notice I've stopped cringing each time an emergency siren seems near. There are too many of them; I'm all cringed out. Coming at me from every possible direction, their grating postindustrial symphony is stuck in permanent crescendo—and built around five or six notes that do not belong in the same scale. I no longer believe this constant wailing has anything to do with me and my terrorist, thinking instead that this, too, is business as usual in a city known for the low median age—and high death rate—of its drug-doling, AK-47–wielding gangsters. Or perhaps, at long last, the police are rounding up all the arms and tobacco merchants, the serious welfare recipients, dragging them kicking and scratching from the public trough.

The sirens remind me that Washington is the per capita cop capital of the world. It is one of the many legacies of a president who gave new meaning to his favorite words, "law and order." But surprisingly, I have yet to see a single dough-nut-dipping representative of the peacekeeping profession. This I consider fortunate, as the police are likely to possess com-puter-generated sketches of me, manifesting every possible variation of facial hair. While the press has settled for exhum-ing the black-and-white photo that appeared on the back jacket, inside flap, of the second hardbound printing of *Cook-book*—the one with the upside-down American flag as a back-drop—the cops will have access to an almost infinite variety of images, one of which is sure to be a simulated photo of a beardless, forty-eight-year-old Rod Huxley.

What I am seeing, more and more, are the foot soldiers in an army of paper-producing, document-digesting profession-als, marching in identical dark suits and identical haircuts and wearing shoes as expensive as all the clothes I own. Fenwick warned me about them somewhere over Iowa. "The pride of Washington," he called them. "You want to feel poor, you just try working where I work. Some of these people make in a day what I make in a year, and they work about as hard as you do."

Deceptively young, these are the consultants, the pollsters and strategists, lobbyists and lawyers—the careerists—drawn to the trough by its stench of power, forever drunk on its pungent rot. I am certain they don't eat at Burger King.

They also do not say "Excuse me" when they try to charge through me on their maneuvers from one air-conditioned fortress to another, their briefcases doubling as battering rams, their arrogance as armor. Why does Fenwick stay in Washington? As far as I was able to tell, he lacks the polish and insincerity, the ruthless determination—traits that seem to be synonymous here with success. Certainly, it's hard to believe Fenwick actually despises his trips for the FBI; it seems more likely he would greet them as welcome escapes. Even I can see he'd be more at home in, say, the agency's South Dakota bureau, where minimal competence could be exchanged for job security and respect, where he could come to work in cowboy boots and those western ties made out of shoelaces. Someday, I strongly suspect, Fenwick will thank me for giving him the ditch and consequently getting him reassigned to such an office.

At last, I reach the living, breathing wall of humanity, still a good city block from the Burger King. K Street, I find, is closed to further pedestrian and automobile traffic, never mind that the latter has already hemorrhaged to a standstill. I turn left and head south, easily passing the venom-spewing delivery-truck drivers and disgruntled, car-addicted commuters who don't know enough to take a subway to work, even on a day like this one.

"Why don't you take a picture?" a teenaged girl loudly inquires, to the delight of her study-hall-skipping companions. "It lasts longer." And this, along with a what-the-fuck-are-you-looking-at stare on the face of a cabbie, reminds me I'm no longer invisible. I turn my head, quicken my pace.

A Manx cat is terrorizing the pigeons of Lafayette Park, just across Pennsylvania Avenue from the White House. Even with its short, pudgy body, the white-and-gray feline is incredibly agile, faster and more graceful than any human athlete, although the cat will never see its name on multi-million-dollar contracts, restaurant menus, or automobile dealership ads.

The grimy brown pigeons scatter, flying in spurts on stubby wings. Only a few minutes ago, tourists who apparently had never seen pigeons before were actually feeding the birds crumbs of bread, ensuring there will be even more winged vermin crowding the park the coming spring.

These camera-clutching, souvenir-scrounging station-wagon owners, I noticed, were not so quick to offer baked goods to the homeless women and children sitting out their daylight hours on the park's cold, concrete benches. It makes me wish the cat weighed a few hundred more pounds, that it was a proud, stealthy panther charging into the tourist horde, sending them diving for cover with their Triple-A guidebooks and Smithsonian Air and Space Museum shopping bags.

But all the cat does is make me think about my own two cats and how worried I am about Darwin and Freud. Now that their owner has reneged on his deal with Special Agent Fenwick, will FBI Denver continue to scoop their poop and refill their yellow plastic water dishes?

Even though I left an open bag of Meow Mix on the floor of my kitchen, I picture Darwin staring at the empty food dish that marks the center of his universe. He spreads his paws without claws, those powerful tools responsible for removing the fabric from the back of my couch; they look huge even next to his stout frame. Darwin is the cat's cat, black with white spats and accents, a jungle creature in his dreams, a house cat against his will. He's rambunctious, clumsy but well meaning, always reaching for doorknobs and freedom or staring out his solitary window through crazed yellow eyes at a world that is rightfully his, where birds and trees delight in taunting him.

Freud is smaller, by way of genetics and temperament. His insecurity makes him a traitor to his species, placing him in constant need of a warm human lap and reassuring hug. He purrs loudly when loved, clutches my finger with his white-mittened paw, a Walt Disney cartoon hand. He's a tabby cat, orange and white, who, unlike Darwin, believes in the status quo. The three rooms of my apartment are all the territory Freud will ever need.

"I know you," a bag lady cries, abruptly returning me to Lafayette Park. "I know you." It is possible she has recognized my face, I realize. Having shared Denver's sidewalks with the dispossessed, I have found them to be fairly well informed, because they read the front page of virtually every newspaper sold in vending boxes.

"I know you," she shouts several more times, before finally easing the tension with, "Poppa, you've come home."

Now this battered survivor—physically if not mentally—of seventy-some difficult years is calling for "Poppa, poppa."

She's attracting the attention of the monument-gawking Midwesterners, along with that of her ragged fellow travelers. I break through the tightening circle and move quickly back toward the north end of the park, to the edge of the police barricades, hoping to avoid recognition by someone who lives on this side of the stratosphere.

H Street, at the north edge of the park, has become the southern boundary of the Buncombese beachhead. According to the people I've asked, the sprawling melee circles the Burger King restaurant like the rings of Saturn, spinning out over an eight-block area, with cops on the inside (I've found them at last), reporters and cops in the middle, and tourists and cops on the outside.

A row of makeshift wooden booths, some of them three or four stories tall, protrudes from the center ring. These turn out to be temporary newsrooms for the three television networks and CNN.

A young reporter is leaving one of the structures. He lugs a blue plastic canister under his left arm. For an instant, I lose sight of him, but now I can see that he's squeezing into and through the outer ring, slowly making his way in my direction. Even in the midst of all this chaos, his perfectly styled hair refuses to budge. The part looks as if it has been measured with precision instruments, then permanently burned into place with lasers.

I do some pushing as well, until I am close enough to this would-be model for an ad promoting a chain of broadcasting correspondence schools to ask if anyone has seen the infamous hippie author in town.

"No, but I wish I had," he half shouts. "I'd love to get a crack at him. Maybe he could explain what's going on here. But fat chance, huh? I doubt if the FBI will let anyone close to him. According to the wire, they should be bringing him in in a few hours. Sorry, Jack, but I've got to run. I've got important stuff to take care of."

So in the interest of saving his own career, Fenwick has done me an enormous favor. He has neglected to tell his fellow Fenwicks about his little lapse. He has given me time and flexibility. And of greatest importance, he has given my cats an extension. Darwin and Freud are being fed, their shit is being scooped. Their litter box cleaning service will not be the first casualty of the BLA October Revolution.

These thoughts keep me from noticing that my elbow is digging into the soft underbelly of a large white Washington, D.C., policeman—until, that is, he asks me brusquely, "You got some business here?"

"No, sir," I reply, pointing to my map. "I'm only trying to find my way to the Smithsonian."

He rolls his eyes as I begin my hasty retreat. It is time to think, time to regroup. It is time to go for a walk.

Seventeenth Street takes me past the Old Executive Office Building and the Ellipse, then gives me my first good look at the Washington Monument. Just inside a rectangle on my map labeled "Constitution Gardens," I discover a beautiful, rolling, tourist-free expanse, green even this late in the year, with wide, manmade ponds and more carefully placed trees.

A second fold of hill reveals the outskirts of the Vietnam Veterans Memorial and—something not on my map—a small, ramshackle shed almost hidden beneath a sprawling "Bring Home the MIAs" banner.

Three vets are manning the booth; they would probably remove the bones from my body if they knew, and remembered, who I was. Even though their war was almost ended by the time my book appeared, my praise of the "heroic defenders of the Vietnamese homeland" had been widely quoted in the straight press, prompting demands for an apology, if not a public execution, from the VFW and American Legion. Mercifully, my assertion that "we are the wolf pack, hiding by day at the city's edge; we are the AmeriCong" had been less widely quoted.

If these vets knew they were staring at "Ho Chi Huxley," as a then unindicted Spiro Agnew had dubbed me, they would pound me into the pavement of Constitution Avenue, then call General Westmoreland to tell him they had added a final name to his wall of shame. (As one of their sleeveless, tattoo-revealing T-shirts argues, "POWs never have a nice day. So why should you?") They would never understand how much they have in common with me.

Like them, I have not allowed my memory to be erased by time and indifference, to be burned away as if by napalm. I still remember the blood and turmoil, remember that the names on the memorial are more than symbols, that those names once belonged to classmates and friends, big brothers and high-school bullies.

Even the pasts of these psychologically disabled vets are more closely aligned with mine than they would have imagined. After all, they were all of eighteen and twenty when the war swallowed them up; they knew as much about defending their country as I knew about saving the world. Our naiveté had been mutual.

Unlike them, however, I would have done anything to keep my pale, cowering body from being herded onto one of Lyndon Baines's transport planes. If my number had come up, I would have gobbled sugar nonstop for a week, fired pistols next to my ear. I would have told the draft tribunal I was gay, and if that didn't work, I would have written them from Canada to say I was no longer a member of the Pax Americana Club.

I keep walking.

"Got any spare change, brother?" a beggar asks. His skin is dark, almost shiny from lack of soap. His face is faintly bearded, a few years older than mine. His breath is borderline toxic, laced with Thunderbird fumes. He looks like he may have failed once at being a hippie, ended up as something less novel, something less romantic. I reach into my pocket and produce a couple of quarters, a nickel or two.

"Thanks, brother. God bless you," he says.

The next beggar gets a twenty-dollar bill from my other pocket. A thin, stubble-chinned black man who would be nearing retirement were he employed, he makes me wonder if it's true that Washingtonians actually went inside a dark theater to watch *Les Misérables*. Poverty and discontent are not things one needs a ticket to see here.

The third supplicant doesn't appear so needy. He approaches me near the stairs at the base of the Lincoln Memorial. "I need money for the bus. My car has broken down."

There are no bus stops in sight, nor broken-down cars, as the area is closed to all traffic apart from tourist buses. On top of that, he's a big guy, in apparent better health than I will ever be. His sunglasses look trendily expensive, and his belt provides a holster for a Walkman cassette player. He doesn't even remove the tiny headphones from his ears when I speak.

"I'd give you something, but you're the third one to ask," I say. "This seems to be a popular location. I have no more change to spare."

"Ho, ho, ho," he bellows as he walks away. "Don't fall for it. You take care of yourself."

The sun is high in the washed-out blue haze. It must be close to twelve, maybe a little after. I cross the Potomac on Memorial Bridge and walk the mile or so to Arlington National Cemetery. Halfway up its hill, surrounded by the patriotic dead, I find a bench, and from it I can see the presidential monuments, exactly as illustrated in the margins of my map. The Kennedy Center. The Jefferson Memorial. The Watergate Hotel. I can see the roof of the Pentagon. Try as I might to deny it, the panorama before me is truly impressive. The rows of manicured trees. The gleaming white buildings, each one a shrine to 3,000 years of Western hubris.

For the first time, I can see why this city draws the idealists as well as the cynics, why they all come here, for tributes and tribulations, in motorcades lit by flashbulbs, or in guilty, shadowy secrecy, the Lincolns and Gorbachevs, the Nixons and the Norths. I'm reminded of the crowd I passed at the Lincoln Memorial, made up of tourists from Japan, South America, and every other landmass on this planet, all here to pay their respects to a man who gave his life to the "proposition that all men are created equal."

The only things out of place in this postcard-in-motion are the police helicopters, circling the Buncombese bastion. They seem far away; from where I sit, they look like gnats drawn to sweat. An American Airlines jet roars overhead—it seems incredibly close—pointing its sleek metal nose toward the runways of an airport hugging the edge of the Potomac.

A wing glares in the sun, and I realize that the light is now coming from just behind my shoulders. It is time. Time to return to Vermont and K and finally face the consequences of my actions. Time to learn how it feels to commit an act of bravery.

CHAPTER 5

"HYPOCRISY DESTROYS MOVEMENT," sniped the lead headline in the *Burning Fist*.

Rad Brad was not pleased with my publishing deal. "Rod Huxley is a dangerous liar," he denounced his former comrade before the world, or at least the Iowa City student community. "He is making it harder to tell our friends from our enemies. At least Nixon is honest with us." Rad, who had stood beside me at the long, folding metal table in the room that doubled as his apartment and *Fist* office, helping me collate 500 books by hand. Rad, who had carried the precious, subversive piles to and from Hawkeye Printers in the back of his Rambler.

"Our biggest problem is that everyone wants their own cult of personality," he concluded in an editorial that took up most of the four-page special issue (twice the length of Rad's previous special issue, "Verdict from the People: Nixon Re-election Declared Illegal"). "Rod Huxley doesn't want to burn down the Bank of Amerika. He wants to deposit his royalties there. John Lennon was right. The dream is over."

The response from my family was predictable. My father called me a communist, a coward, and five other things that started with C.

"I don't care if much of the book was, as you say, out of your control," he bellowed. "Your name is the one I see on its cover, and that is something you cannot change, although I suspect there will be days when you wish that could be so."

Things improved when I received my first royalty check.

"It's a shame you didn't register for my classes at DCC," he told me over the phone. "You would have learned some vital investment skills." I offered him 15% to manage my tainted earnings. The deal was sealed: Benton Huxley was now my financial advisor. It was the first time—to my knowledge, at least—that I had given him something he even remotely appreciated.

My older brother called me a bum with a bankroll. "You've finally done it," Tyler phoned to scold me. "You've embarrassed our family on a national scale. At least we can hold our heads up in Russia and North Vietnam."

Years earlier, when my brother was not yet ashamed to show his face in the country of his birth, a family vacation had taken us to the Royal Gorge, about two hours south of my present Denver home. As we discovered, the narrow Arkansas River had cut a deep groove into the primeval earth, exposing millions of years of geologic records, revealing copper-red rocks that had once supported the weight of dinosaurs, and leaving me reeling from the incredible, time-compressing plunge. It was all too magnificent, and my brain hurt from trying to process too much sensory information.

"Times like these make you wish you were a poet or an artist," Tyler boldly pronounced.

When I reminded him that I was a tormented young genius, he laughed disparagingly.

"You won't laugh when I'm on the best-seller list," I suggested.

He was howling by then, however. "Now, that is true," he conceded. "I won't be laughing if that happens." He was playing the role of big brother. It was something he did well.

When Tyler graduated with a B.S. in economics from DCC, a huge accounting firm in Omaha was quick to hire him as a labor affairs specialist. His job was to doctor the annual reports of corporations that had previously rewarded their stock-holders with intoxicating tales of unchecked growth and record profit. Tyler's task was to revise the documents for the purpose of one-sided contract negotiations with the laboring masses. Like an evil alchemist, he turned the black ink into red; he made profits disappear, producing alternate reports that showed huge losses and looming bankruptcies. These, needless to say, were ideal for sanctioning the draining of pension accounts and the cutting of hourly wages.

He described his job in detail when he and I went home for Christmas in December 1971. This was the first time I'd met his clinging Nebraska bride, Trudy. She was thin even next to my gangly brother, looked as if she might become translucent were someone to place her in front of a glaring spotlight.

"Face it," Tyler argued while Trudy beamed approvingly. "Those overpaid John Deere workers are the first ones to apply for food stamps when they get laid off. The company hands them money and they spend it on boats, beer, and second cars. They don't save a penny. The company might as well reinvest that money into their future."

"By giving it to some blood-sipping stockholder who's never even stepped inside a John Deere plant?" I asked.

"The shareholders are more important to the company's survival than the laborers," he replied, startling me with his sincerity. "I mean, come on, Rod, what would you know about stepping into a factory? Workers are easily replaced. They come and go. But you just go ahead, you take all the investors and lawyers and accountants outside and line them up and shoot them, see what you've got left. Who's going to make sure everyone else is doing the work? And if no one owns the factory, where are they going to work in the first place?"

One year later, no one even proposed getting together for the holidays. The publication of *Cookbook* had made sure of that. "I'm not going all the way to Hanoi," Tyler groused over the phone. "You know—where your real family lives." I sent him a present anyway: an autographed copy of the first paperback printing, with the *Ramparts* blurb on its cover.

"A young couple can never have enough *Cookbooks*," I'd inscribed on the title page.

"I hope this reaches you in time," Aaron Hamilton Scott III typed in his first letter, dated February 2, 1973. "Let this small contribution keep you out of jail and on the streets, where you can work your good. Power to the protesters. We will prevail. Death to the $ystem."

His check said more than the letter, of course—about $400,000 more—as it officially introduced me to the patronage system. In an instant, Rod Huxley, stalwart foe of wealth in need of redistribution, had become both rich and confused.

"What does he want in return?" I asked Sara. "I must be taking on some sort of debt. And since when are revolutionaries supposed to have money? I showed you that editorial from the *New York Times*. I've already been labeled an 'armchair activist' and 'cheerleader come lately.' What will be expected of me now?"

"But isn't this basically good?" Sara asked. "Now you can take all the time you want to write, about anything you want. Does it really matter so much where this money came from, or even that Moss helped you write some of your first book? Think of the money as a grant, a grant toward doing the books we both know are in your future."

My new brothers and comrades—all of them—had better plans for spending my grant.

"It's time we put Rod's book into action," said Red Vince as he convened the meeting of the revolutionary cell. "It's time we actually did some cooking."

"How about the chapter on 'freeing the free press'?" Carlos suggested. "We could seize the means of communication. Shades of 1917."

"Yeah, we could take over the Iowa City television station."

"Naw, that's a public education channel," Lonny X dissented. "No one watches."

It was noted that the only strategic network station was WMT in Cedar Rapids. "We're talking a thirty-minute drive, max. We could easily go up there and take it over."

"No way, man," Carlos sneered. "Cedar Rapids smells bad, with all its factories and dumps. It's no place to start the Revolution. Man, it's no place to spend a weekend, believe me. Talk about a downer."

Red Vince suggested burning down the Iowa City *Press Citizen* offices, then taking over the *Burning Fist*. "There's only one truth. There should be only one paper in this town. Like *Pravda* in Russia, man."

Red Vince was a speed-freak chemistry student who had entered college some ten years earlier with a goal of "making my own acid and bombs." He had since come to realize that the destruction of Western civilization would erase all records of his numerous student loans. Red boasted that he had been a communist since he was six, when an elementary-school teacher told his class about a place where children snitched on their parents. "I wanted to live there."

Befitting his name of choice, Red's hair, an orange afro of sorts, looked as if it had been set afire. A thousand tiny flames shot out in every direction, like the sun's corona on overdrive. This, needless to say, added to the overall image of dementia. "You know what I'd really love to do?" he once shared with me. "I'd love to walk into Chicago's Art Institute and destroy every piece-of-shit thing I could get close to. I'd douse all the paintings with kerosene. Turn marble to dust. Bye, bye,

Rembrandt. Fuck you, Mary Cassatt. That, brother, would be art. A literal break with the past, like you prescribed in *Cookbook*."

"I don't recall that passage," I confessed.

The personal revelation Lonny X chose to unload on me had to do with the "Jap exchange students" who also roomed in his ten-dollar-a-week tenement dwelling. "They're stealing my socks from the laundry-room dryers," he said.

Lonny X introduced himself to anyone who was or wasn't interested as a "black Muslim." Never mind that he looked more like a white Methodist (or that in the past year alone, he'd been a two-time fraternity reject, Up with People roadie, and charter member of the Rhadha Krishna Temple, Iowa City). He wore reddish-brown penny loafers, complete with the appropriate coins. His wheat-colored hair barely touched the tops of his disproportionately large ears, which sprang from his head like car doors swinging open. His Mao badge was so small as to be almost invisible.

"We need to think bigger," Carlos said. "We set up a people's government here in Iowa City, offer asylum to Allende ('cause you know he's fucked). We bring Timothy Leary and George McGovern here. Maybe Jane Fonda. It wouldn't hurt to have a good-looking broad to help out. Did anyone see *Barbarella*? Man, I'd go to Hanoi with her in a second."

Sara, the only sister in our revolutionary cell—and the only person paying rent on the apartment in which we met—voiced her disapproval. "Excuse me for existing, but—"

"I don't want to hear that chauvinist rap again, Sar' honey," Carlos cut her off. "So don't start."

I noted that when Carlos took the floor, his speech and behavior usually matched his appearance, which was that of a shadowy, sinister figure. He was older than the rest of us, late thirties at the youngest, and his psychology-textbook intensity made me realize he had used his head start in life to completely bury the rest of us, Red Vince included, in per capita consumption of drugs and alcohol. "I was in the Haight," he'd once claimed, "before the hangers-on and weekend hippies bled the scene dry." With his dark hair and dark skin—a twenty-year-old suntan turned to leather—he looked remarkably like the logo on packets of Zig Zag cigarette papers.

Carlos, appropriately, had come to Iowa City as part of a group called the Yappies. Officially, they were the Students for Nonattainable Proletarian Democracy, and they had converged upon the Pentacrest green for their Year One International Summit. This took place during my first semester in the Writers' Workshop. I had gone to their summit as an observer, intending to study successful revolutionary techniques. Sara had been there, too, watching the show.

That placed us well within the majority. Because for every Yappie there were nine curious onlookers, and the crowd numbered only about 100. Still, the Yappies made a lot of noise that night, running in stoned circles while singing "We all live in a concentration camp" to the chorus of "Yellow Submarine" and giving credence to the rumor that even the yippies couldn't stand them. As we'd been warned by the stories that preceded their arrival, the Yappies had actually been thrown out of the yippies for being too obnoxious.

More than a year later, Carlos was keeping that legacy alive. "I'm not talking more tokenism," he contended, further demonstrating his unique ability to infuriate Sara. "Jane Fonda would be useful here. She could narrate propaganda films or something, help promote the message of peace and revolution." Carlos was wearing one of his homemade headbands, which resembled nothing so much as the elastic strip from a pair of discarded underwear, and it made his long, oily hair even flatter and straighter as it plummeted to his narrow shoulders. What it didn't do was argue effectively for his notions of male superiority. "Maybe Jane could lure Peter here, along with Dennis Hopper. He seems like a pretty cool guy."

Sara got up and walked to the refrigerator, ostensibly to refill her empty wine glass. Carlos took no notice.

"Yeah, fantastic. We declare a New International." It was Lonny X again. "We establish relations with Hanoi, declare our political solidarity."

Lazlo Roach, a very withdrawn fourth-year university freshman who, even as he sat on the American flag we used as a throw rug, was withdrawing further into a fuzzy ball of hair and marijuana smoke, kept repeating in a spooky half whisper, "Up against the wall, motherfuckers."

As if on cue, the wall behind me started to vibrate. The football players were home from practice. *"Shaft. He's a bad mother."* It was the Isaac Hayes soundtrack album, a current favorite of two brothers who happened to be "brothers," each of whom was built like a massive, lumpy snowman with the bottom sections reversed. On another afternoon, I'd been told, Lonny X had approached the pair, no doubt with his threadbare "¿Que pasa?" and clenched-fist salute, inviting them to "join the Revolution." "So you rich white boys are planning to take over the world?" came the response. "That'll be something new."

Shaft's bass notes rattled the light fixtures, along with three wax-coated candleholders on the bathroom sink. But there wasn't much else to disturb in Sara's apartment. She owned only a few dishes and glasses—and two cereal bowls that actually matched. Of six pieces of silverware, four were spoons. Earlier that spring, she had turned down a free-for-the-lugging sofa bed and beanbag chair from an old dorm mate who was being evicted. Although she may have passed on the furniture solely to irritate Carlos, who often complained about having to sit on the hardwood floor, Sara Caine was a true antimaterialist, perhaps the only one I'd known who could denounce hypocrisy and greed without making herself a hypocrite in the process. Apart from her lopsided stacks of paperback books, their titles unrecognizable from the wear on their spines, her possessions included a mattress, desk, and single chair (the refrigerator and stove belonged to the landlord). She didn't even count a stereo among her limited holdings.

"My radio gives me plenty of choice," she explained to me once. "I'm a fan of music, not individual musicians. Whatever song I'm listening to becomes my favorite. Besides, how can anyone own music?"

These statements were so typical of Sara—the kind that made me genuinely admire her, even while annoying the absolute hell out of me. At times, I was tempted to corrupt her by procuring a stereo for the apartment, one with hulking JBL speaker cases and a fifty-watt amp, especially now that her neighbors had tired of Marvin Gaye and Stevie Wonder. "There, now you own music," I would tell Sara, while producing a selection of my own favorite albums, the covers still gleaming in their factory shrink-wrap.

I feared, however, I'd be tempting Lonny X to share his Seals and Crofts collection. And I wasn't even curious to know what kind of music Red Vince preferred.

"What if we faked Rod's death?" Carlos was asking. "Laid it at the hands of the CIA and FBI. Then we'd have a martyr to rally around. We could march toward Washington, growing in number as we went. Just walk in and take the city, like that, without a lot of bloodshed."

"There can be no successful peaceful revolution," Red Vince enlivened the discussion with an opinion he had stated before, on other endless afternoons. "Look at Gandhi. He should have killed the British, killed the Muslims, then killed any Hindus who disagreed even slightly with his views. There's no chance of retaliation that way—the Revolution is secure—

and there's a lot more wealth to divvy up among the masses, or what's left of them."

"This is not what I had in mind when I wrote my book," I spoke up at last. "We can't exterminate everyone we differ with. Even if we all surrendered our ability to reason and agreed with Red Vince, do you have any idea how many guns are out there? I think we would quickly learn who owns the police forces and the military, the weapons of private property. We wouldn't have a chance."

"Sorry, man, but it *is* all in your book," Red Vince snarled. "Besides, what's the point of having a revolution if we can't have a purge or two? I've got enemies, you know."

Lonny X narrowed his eyes. "Yeah, Rod. If you've got something better in mind, then don't keep it from us. Lead us. We're waiting."

"Yeah, free love, free drugs," mumbled Lazlo Roach.

"From the barricades to the guillotines," Red Vince was only a few decibels shy of shouting. "It's a natural progression. And it's the only way to get rid of all these plastic politicians and straights." I kept my eyes on his bottle of Southern Comfort to see if he'd send it flying with an involuntary whack, as he often did when his seizures of anger peaked. "I say we bust open the Anamosa Correctional Facility, take the inmates, and form an army that will devour everything in its path. Like locusts, man. Like fucking Spartacus and his slave rebellion."

"That's insane," I said.

"That's from your *Cookbook for Revolution,*" Red Vince snapped. "'Free the prisoners, jail the judges.' Are you sure you're the same Rod Huxley who wrote our manifesto?"

"But all this talk of unrestrained violence . . ."

"Jesus, man, go read your book." His arm came within inches of the Southern Comfort. "I mean, what's the fucking hang here? Did you wake up on the wrong side of thirty this morning?" Whacked at last, the bottle banged and bounced and skidded like a rocket tipped sideways at launch, all the while leaking its pungent, highly flammable fuel.

Carlos looked up at Sara, now leaning against the kitchen door frame, letting her know which gender was expected to deal with spills.

This was something she'd stopped doing many weeks before.

"Perhaps we're losing perspective," Sara spoke calmly, doing her best to ignore Carlos—and the other, less offensive mess on her floor. "We need something practical as our goal, something that might be, at the very least, physically possible. I think some of us are missing the point of Rod's book."

It was at that moment Lazlo Roach suggested a bee-in.

"A be-in?" Red Vince objected. "You're talking ancient history. They were doing the be-in scene in San Francisco five years ago. We don't need to go backwards in time. Sorry, brother, but peace and love won't play here."

"No, man, a *bee*-in. B-e-e–in. This dealer friend of mine's got a farm for growing pot, down by Mount Pleasant. His old man used to keep bees there. Anyway, Mouse hasn't had the time or motivation to take care of the hives, so the bees are kinda overrunning the place. He'd love to get rid of them, so I suggest we take them off his hands and put them to work against the Man. Don't you see? We'll sic the bees on the pigs."

"Yeah, yeah. We get some protective clothing—"

"Mouse already has the beekeeper outfits," Roach said.

"And where is this to take place?" I asked.

"How about the Selective Service office?" suggested Lonny X.

"I think it's closed now that the draft's gone," Red Vince noted, his rage temporarily checked. "And even when it was open here, that office was basically an old woman and a chair. It wouldn't have taken too many bees to shut it down."

"You're in the right building, at least," Roach said, now clearly on a roll. "But I'll tell you where we do it. The post office."

"The post office?"

"Yeah, Lazlo, the post office?"

"Don't you see, man? It's the cardiovascular system of Amerika." Lazlo Roach was becoming absolutely enthusiastic as his plan was revealed. "It's the heart, the vessels, the arteries." His eyes, though still partially obscured by a permanent THC glaze, were actually shining. "Where is all the wealth transferred from the have-nots to the haves through an endless flow of taxes and bills? Where are the FBI's Most Wanted posters, framing our brothers in the Movement? You want to look into the eyes of the oppressor at close range, the post office is the place to go. Man, it's pig central."

"So how does this start the Revolution?" asked Sara.

"With gangrene, as opposed to a blood clot," Roach explained. "Our cadres in other cities will copy our actions, dig? Let it spread through the veins until it closes down the whole motherfucking system. You gotta know the working class will rise up, once they've been deprived of their *Playboys*, *Reader's Digests*, and *Popular Mechanics*. Then, it's up against the wall, motherfuckers. I tell you, it can't miss."

Shaking the sleep from my legs, I pushed myself up and lumbered to the apartment's front door, then cracked it open to let in some fresh, cool air—a less-than-even exchange for our fetid blend of bourbon fumes, reefer, strawberry incense, and the bearlike scent of four men who passionately disbelieved in cologne and deodorant. I glimpsed a couple playing Frisbee, pictured me and Sara in their places, my partner shielding her eyes from the late-afternoon sun.

"Right on, Roach." Carlos had picked up some of Lazlo's enthusiasm. "We dress like beekeepers, which will be cool in itself because we'll probably look like something out of a B movie about space aliens. Then, we crash the post office sorting room, with each of us holding a jar of bees. We throw our Molotov buzz bombs onto the floor and watch the Revolution start. It'll be amazing."

"That's the silliest idea I ever heard," I said, reclaiming my place on the floor. I was certain, for once, that most of the others would be in agreement with me.

"Yeah, but I like it. It's kind of Monty Pythonish."

"Monty Python is television, Lonny," I reminded my comrade. "We're talking about real people here, some of whom may not be fond of bee stings."

"Ah, screw you. The racist-genocidal war the government is conducting against my brothers from Africa is television, man. Vietnam is fucking television. And my name is Lonny X."

I said, "During the past three months, I've listened to embryonic plans for eliminating automobile pollution by dumping nails onto the streets. I've listened to RedVince push for commandeering a nuclear missile silo. Or how about kidnapping the ex-Beatles and forcing them to record and perform together, at gunpoint, for the Revolution?"

"It was better than Lonny X's idea we kidnap everyone who played at Woodstock."

"That's not the point, Carlos," I said. "The point is that none of these proposals has made sense. And now, a bee-in? It's as if we're trying to parody ourselves. I'm sorry, but if that's the best plan we can devise, I'm out."

"You've been saying that for weeks now, Huxster," Red Vince sneered, borrowing a nickname recently given me by Rad Brad. "If you're not for the Movement, you're for the status quo. You're goddamn Henry Kissinger. For someone who claims to be for toppling the tyrants and warmongers, you are one hung-up dude. Why did you write *Cookbook for*

Revolution? That's assuming it's even true you were the one who wrote it."

Red Vince had one last question, but it wasn't for me. "Hey, Roach, about your beekeeper dealer friend. You think he could score me some white cross?"

These people frightened me, and in doing that, they pushed me closer to the one person I could trust.

"Sara, have you been listening to our little band of psychopaths? You can't tell me Red Vince actually desires a better world, only a world where he is the supreme, unquestioned ruler. Unfortunately, his agenda clashes with the one privately held by Carlos, which gives Carlos that same prize. We should be glad a bee-in is the best they've come up with. It can't possibly fly."

Still, I knew I couldn't talk Sara out of her role in the Iowa City People's Bee-In for Peace and Revolution. Although she would not be carrying her own jar of stinging insects, she would accompany the others to help them avoid injury and arrest, the latter by facilitating the getaway—a role that fell often to revolutionary sisters.

"So maybe Vince and Carlos are not exactly sane," she said, "and maybe drugs and revolution don't mix very well. But until a better idea for bringing down the system comes along, at least Lazlo and the others are doing something. They're not just complaining."

"It's too damned convenient," I said, "too black and white, defining ourselves by a common enemy. But the worst of it is, Red Vince is correct. It was all in my *Cookbook,* right from the start. I can't even blame Moss. I was the one who encouraged this nonsense."

CHAPTER 6

A PAIR OF CONCRETE LIONS, stationed at the Washington end of Arlington Memorial Bridge, defends the Lincoln Memorial from marauding Virginians. Like the giant marble president they serve, the lions make me think about courage—and how little of it seems to run in my family. As much as I hate to admit it, I find myself agreeing with what surely would be my father's appraisal of heroism. It is too risky, too disruptive. If it weren't, more people would be willing to try it.

I buy the cheapest souvenir I can find in the Memorial gift shop: a "Lincoln Emancipates the Slaves" keychain. I now have two quarters for the pay phone outside.

My first call—to Information—is free. "Thanks for your help," I say, but the operator has already moved on to her next anonymous five-second encounter. (Apparently, the cost of paying an employee to say "You're welcome" is one Bell Atlantic cannot afford, not with their adjusted-for-inflation union wages.) I deposit a coin, quickly dial the number I'm repeating in my head.

"You have reached the offices of *The Washington Post*. If you know your extension, you may enter that number now." I feel prechewed gum forming a seal between my ear and the phone. At least, I hope it's gum. "If you need to speak to an operator, press zero or stay on the—"

"*Washington Post*. How may I direct your call?"

"I have important information for your national affairs department."

"One second, please."

There is a ring, followed by another cold, flat recording. "You have reached the desk of Damon Drummond. If you wish to leave a message, please do so at the sound of the beep. You may press zero at any time to return to—"

"*Washington Post.*"

"Operator, it's me again. Now listen carefully. This is Rod Huxley. You'll find me on page one of today's edition. I have information for which any reporter in this city would offer up his family in trade. Is there anyone who could help me?"

"How about our desk for community law enforcement oversight?"

"What's that? Police beat?"

"As you wish."

"But . . ."

Five rings and a click. "Bob Neville, community law enforcement oversight."

"This is Rod Huxley. I have the ultimate scoop for you, but I need something in return. I'll tell you anything you want to know if you can arrange a meeting for me with the Burger King terrorist, free of FBI interference. I'll also need assurance that my cats are still receiving adequate care."

"Just one second." I am put on hold for more than a minute. Then, "Joke's over."

"This is no joke. The FBI is lying. This is Rod Huxley. I need to get into the Burger King."

"If that's so, why wouldn't you trust the feds to take you in?"

"The agent they assigned to me gets on my nerves. I can't think in his presence. Together, we're destined to screw things up."

"Is this Feurste? Come on, man, I've only had this job for three weeks. Quit fucking with me."

"This isn't Feurste, goddammit. This is Rod Huxley. *The* Rod Huxley. I need your help."

A Vietnam vet the shape and size of an older-model refrigerator now waits to use the phone. He's wearing a green beret, a purple heart, too; I don't think I'll be dropping my name again.

"Maybe I should transfer you to Woodward and Bernstein," Neville is saying. "Oh, wait a minute. What's that, Carl? You've already filed your once-in-a-lifetime story? Look, pal, why don't you call the *Washington Times,* ask for Reverend Moon. They specialize in bullshit."

"This isn't bullshit."

"Yeah, whatever. I suggest you get over your fear of the FBI and leave me alone. They're the ones who set up kook lines for this sort of thing."

"Listen, you stupid young shit, you're throwing away what is likely to be the only opportunity in an otherwise limited future."

"Excuse me, Mr. Huxley, but Patricia Hearst's on my other line."

Silence, at least from the *Post.*

"Hey, man," the vet charges swiftly into this void, "what the fuck are you doing!?"

This is an understandable reaction. For what I am doing is hanging up a phone with the force required to hammer a nail into concrete.

"I need to use that thing," the vet tells me. "That's why I've been standing here so fucking patiently." He moves closer. "Hey, do I know you?" He's holding a copy of the *Washington Times.* My full-color photo takes up most of the front page.

"Sorry. Here's a quarter to make your call." I throw in the keychain, too. "I should know better than to rely on phones. I've never had much luck with these things."

"Yeah, that's what I was thinking. 'Cause I right away took you for one of them big power-lunch types. You and your Fortune 500 buddies staring each other down as you wrap up another billion-dollar deal. Thanks for the quarter. The phone had better work."

When B-Day came, I was hiding in the single room I rented from an elderly widow on Market Street. But even hiding proved impossible.

"You've got a phone call, Mr. Huxley," my landlady called up to me.

I hurried down the stairs, expecting to hear an update on the bee-in from Sara.

"Huxley, how the hell are you?"

"Moss."

"How's everything in the Underground? Overthrown any empires lately? Look, I'm calling because I have a proposal you need to consider. It's a movie deal. Some Hollywood money merchants want to turn our *Cookbook* into a movie. Make it a light comedy, with a plot. Do it fast and cheap. Personally, I think they're making a mistake, because I was right—it was a fad and it's over. But that doesn't mean we can't take their money. It just means no one will pay to see their stupid movie when it's finished."

He added, "It really is a shame old Uncle Sam ended the draft when he did. We could have sold more books and subsequently racked up a few more digits on this movie deal. But as it is now, the market has dwindled. Suddenly, all these Spocked-up white kids who were making so much noise have nothing to whine about. Their own butts are safe, and if you think they care about anything else besides getting a job that will pay them more than they're worth when they get out of college, you're even crazier than I thought. Not that you can complain, Huxley. At least you got to play author for a while."

After a brief pause, he asked, "So what do you think? 'Dustin Hoffman is Rod Huxley in *Cookbook for Revolution*'? Okay, so it might be William Shatner. You won't have to lift a finger. They already have a screenwriter on hold. All you need to do is give me an answer, because they need one, as in pronto."

"I'll think about it," I promised Moss, and I did, too, for all of thirty seconds.

"Have you heard any news?"

Sara was fairly buzzing as I opened the door to let her into my room.

"No, what happened?" I asked.

"What didn't happen? It was a disaster. A certifiable disaster. Not everyone made it back. We lost Lazlo Roach."

"Lost him?"

"It was chaos from the start," Sara said. "When we first stormed the sorting room, which wasn't all that hard to do, Lonny X attempted to lead everyone in song. He was wailing, 'All we are saying, is give bees a chance.' No one joined him, however, and his only accompaniment was the sound of glass breaking as four half-gallon jars hit the floor. In an instant, there were bees everywhere. Then, to everyone's amazement and shock, there were gunshots being fired. That's right. One of the workers was trying to defend himself against the bees. Who would have thought postal employees carried guns to work?"

"Jesus, what happened next?"

"For starters, Red Vince was acting like he'd been stung a few too many times. He was yelling, 'This is for Attica, you bastards!' He was practically spitting through the screen that shielded his face, screaming at workers who were only inches away. There was this one poor kind-of-matronly-looking woman; you could tell she just wanted to finish her sorting and go home. But Vince wouldn't let up, and neither would the bees. And if that wasn't weird enough, a few of the customers waiting in line for window service began cheering. One old guy was shouting—I mean, shouting at the top of his lungs—'Serves you right, you lazy, loafing government lackeys.'"

I had never seen Sara so animated, so charged with nervous energy. "It was unbelievable. And now that Lonny had an actual opening, he initiated a communal chant: 'One, two, three, four, we don't want your mail no more!' This kept us from noticing that Lazlo had chained himself to one of those big carts full of mail. But someone else had noticed—a resourceful postal clerk. And he, in turn, came up with the idea of running into his break room and buying a few bottles of Coca-Cola."

She started to sit on the edge of my bed, but she didn't appear to actually touch the mattress. In an instant she was back on her feet, pacing from one part of my room to another as she talked. "When the clerk returned, he instructed two of his co-workers to yank the headgear from Lazlo's beekeeper suit. Once that was taken care of, the clerk poured the first bottle of Coke down into the suit. Then he violently shook each of the remaining bottles, one at a time, holding his thumb over their mouths, and pointed them at Lazlo. Even before the first bottle had released all of its spray and foam, Lazlo was wearing a body-length suit of bees. He was flailing his bee-covered arms, and his screams were painful to hear. Lazlo jumped into the cart, disappearing from our sight. Meanwhile, the postal workers were moving fast. A few of them grabbed the edge of the cart and rolled it out onto the dock and into the back of a waiting semi trailer. One shouted at a driver, 'Get the hell out of here!'"

"But Lazlo's all right, isn't he?" I asked. "Christ, I knew someone would get hurt."

"The last we saw of Lazlo was a buzzing, writhing, human-shaped blur sticking out of the cart as the truck raced away. Except for the envelopes and cards sticking to Lazlo's beekeeper suit, I knew that what I was witnessing was very much like watching someone who had been sprayed from head to toe with napalm. It must have felt like it, too, because, again, it was painful to listen to Lazlo's cries."

"One symbolic act does not cancel out a history of treachery," Rad Brad railed in his lead editorial, "Bee Gone, Huxster." "And the Iowa City Bee-In, however brilliant the strategy, seems less the action of a true revolutionary and more that of a duplicitous pseudo-visionary out to burn his so-called brothers by hustling a few more books for profit."

Below a hazy gray-and-white photograph taken from a four-year-old student identification card, the caption read, "Lazlo Roach: No sacrifice too great for a true revolutionary."

Unfortunately, before the B-Day debacle, I had committed myself to one final act of self-promotion, and it proved to be a sin that carried its own built-in punishment. With a little prodding from some faceless publicist in the Meiser & Grubb marketing department, I had consented to appear on *Writers' Bloc,* a half-hour television series produced by the Iowa City public television station.

The prodding continued even after I agreed to do the show. "If it's a success, we'll send a tape of the program to other educational channels," I was told over the phone. "Mr. Moss says it will rekindle sales."

B-Day came and went. My reluctance turned to dread.

"We've got big plans for this if you pull it off," another of M & G's marketing specialists called to remind me the afternoon before the broadcast. "And remember, Mr. Moss wants you to announce the movie deal. On the air. He says you've run out of time. They need an answer now."

"Maybe I don't believe in selling out," I confronted Moss's lackey.

"Yeah, and maybe you'd like to return the money we've already sent you. Mr. Moss handed you that book. It's hardly a secret here. It's time for the payback."

"We're 'freeing the free press,' man," said Lonny X, slapping me on the shoulder as I left Sara's apartment on my way to the studio. "Do it for the Roach, Rod."

None of my comrades appeared to mind that the show would be carried locally only, on the channel "no one watched."

"We'll be with you in revolutionary spirit," Carlos assured me.

My credibility had been temporarily restored by the impending television appearance—and because it had been my plan that enabled everyone but true revolutionary Lazlo Roach to escape from the post office without facing arrest. What the others failed to grasp is that I had come up with that plan out of concern for Sara, and Sara only.

For two weeks leading up to B-Day, my Xeroxed notice had been posted in feed-and-seed stores throughout Johnson County. "BEEKEEPERS: The United States Department of Agriculture has determined that potentially toxic substances were used in the making of all beekeeper suits currently in use," it began. "At 11 A.M. on Tuesday, May 1, 1973, you are urged to trade in your present suits for new, improved outfits. In addition to being safer, these revolutionary new suits are lighter and less restricting. Additionally, they are less expensive to manufacture, and thus, the Department of Agriculture will be giving all participating beekeepers a $100 refund." I added this line because I knew Iowa farmers were likely to be skeptical of any government report on "toxic" materials. "Due to expected volume, the exchange will take place in the main lobby of the Iowa City Federal Building, 28 South Linn, First Floor. Remember to bring your suits."

And so it was that at precisely 11 A.M. on May 1, Sara Caine led the surviving members of the B-Day Five out of the sorting room and into the main lobby. Carlos found the remaining jar—the getaway jar, the one that would have been mine—right where he'd left it, next to the water cooler. While a few dozen puzzled farmers watched, Carlos gave it a determined kick. And as that jar exploded against the opposite wall, the beekeepers went for their suits.

Within seconds, there were, by Sara's estimate, twenty fully outfitted beekeepers ready to tear the Federal Building to the ground, one stone at a time, looking for answers. And this is what the Iowa City Police encountered when they arrived on the scene: a horde of ornery Iowa beekeepers, as stubborn and confused as the bees that had been liberated by the Revolution.

"Looks like a college prank," the officer in charge noted. "One that seems to have been exaggerated by our dispatcher.

"Get moving," he said next. "All of you. Go back to your dorms and study for your finals. We don't have time for your games today."

The B-Day conspirators walked to their van. The farmers refused to budge and were ultimately arrested.

My political resurrection was short-lived.

"Welcome to *Writers' Bloc*. Our guest today is radical author Rod Huxley," a disembodied voice announced over the studio's internal public address system. "And, filling in for our usual host, Brent Felcher, is the respected author and head of the University of Iowa's prestigious Fiction Writers' Workshop, Mr. Ernest Luther Gripp."

"Mr. Huxley, you grew up in eastern Iowa in the Mississippi River valley," Gripp began, unleashing the voice that required no P.A. system. "This is rich soil for literature, Mark Twain country. Why, then, don't we see this in your writing?

Why don't you incorporate some of your own experiences, if you have indeed had any, into your writing?"

"The Mississippi River is a ditch in the center of the Amerikan wasteland, a conduit for poisons and pollution," I said without conviction, and with even less concentration. "As for my place of birth, Dubuque was a great place to grow up, and a great place to leave behind. I have no interest in digging up memories that took me years to bury. My writings concern the future, not the past."

"Mr. Huxley, someday in that future, this will be a bad memory, I assure you. It seems to me a writer must have a body of experiences from which to draw. It seems to me you have drawn your inspiration from a dictionary of this year's clichés. Have you ever considered living a few more years, perhaps, then writing about that experience?"

He did not let me answer.

"Moving forward, I suppose we could discuss the merits of your writing, but that would make for a very brief show. So let's instead focus on the message of your book. Mr. Huxley, your *Cookbook for Revolution* doesn't offer specific plans for overthrowing the 'system' that so annoys and represses its author. Why is this?"

"Perhaps you need to read the book, sir," I said, not believing I had called him "sir."

"I have read the book, unfortunately, and I repeat my question: where is your plan—your suggestions and instructions—for revolution?"

I looked to my right. The large black-and-white clock, an acid-free flashback to a million high-school study halls, was broken; it had to be, because its hands had not moved since the inquisition began.

"Then perhaps you could enlighten me regarding another troublesome point, Mr. Huxley. What is it you stand for— apart, obviously, from tossing our great heritage of English literature onto the scrap pile? Are you for anything whatsoever, or are you simply against everything?"

I don't remember how I responded to these queries, don't recall if Gripp followed them with more questions. What I do remember is falling, tumbling helplessly into a dark, bottomless void—the very sensation I'd experienced on the day of the bee-in, when I briefly considered joining my comrades at the post office. This time, my rescue came from an unlikely source, when the esteemed workshop director stepped in to break my descent.

"Huxley, are you all right?" he whispered, shaking my wrist.

"Is it over?"

Gripp pointed to the fuzzy-gray monitor, now devoted entirely to a seven-digit number.

"*Writers' Bloc* welcomes the opinions of its viewers," the invisible announcer explained. "The number on your screen is that of our direct studio line. It is time now to take your calls."

The first two were supportive.

"Right on, brother. I stole a copy of your book at the campus store, and all I can say is, well, right on."

"The racist military-industrial complex controls our thoughts through radio waves directed at the mercury in our dental fillings. Your book shines a beam of truth through the radio-wave fog. You tell it like it is. No lies, no obfuscation. Obviously, you have never visited a dentist."

I recognized the third voice at once.

"Do you feel hypocrisy is undermining our movement?" Rad Brad demanded to know. "If we can't trust our friends, how can we trust self-proclaimed leaders like Rod Huxley? As we've learned from our Marxist comrades abroad, these cults of personality are reactionary and destructive. They run counter to the movement of history. My question for Rod

Huxley is this: would he rather burn down the Bank of Amerika or deposit his money there?"

Now I was certain the clock had stopped running.

"Thank you for your calls," Gripp said. "Your comments and questions were most revealing." Not surprisingly, he couldn't resist finishing me off while I was doubled over, dazed and gasping for breath. "Echoing the skepticism of the last caller," he circled in, "I, too, am curious to know who it is that will lead this new utopian society into the future. Tell me, Mr. Huxley, am I looking at that leader?"

Inexplicably perhaps, I wanted to tell Gripp the truth, if only to terminate my ordeal, like a child yelling "Uncle!" to surrender in a fistfight.

I wanted to explain that a funny thing had happened since my book was published: the fire had gone out. Where previously there had been raging, uncontrollable fury, now there was only smoke. Of course, Clifford Moss had already successfully contained its flames, pissing on it with his stream of endless revisions, with his drippy humor and watered-down words. This made it easy for Red Vince and all the rest to come along and douse what was left.

I wanted to talk, too, about Rad Brad and Lazlo Roach. Perhaps compose some sort of apology.

But what I said was, "I am a fake. I am a fake. I am a fake." At least, I heard myself saying this, almost unconsciously, a confession turned mantra.

Finally, "There is no Revolution. There will be no Revolution."

Walking from the studio to Sara's Summit Street apartment, I visited a barbershop for the first time in more years than I could remember, making a permanent stranger of the longhaired prophet of social reconstruction on the jacket of my book.

"New look," was all Sara said at first. She was the only one waiting for me.

"Where are the disciples?" I asked.

"Gone," she said.

"As in, for good?"

"For good. Carlos said he was no longer in favor of *faking* your death. Lonny then suggested they vote to disband the revolutionary cell."

"Fuck voting," had been Red Vince's response. "Let's get out of here."

"You know Jane Fonda would never take this from her man," Carlos had needled Sara on his way out the door. "You sure you don't want to come with us, Sar'?"

"Right on! I see my contribution helped keep you out of jail," the second letter from Aaron Hamilton Scott III began. It was dated September 5, 1973. "If you need any more capitali$t collateral for your legal defense, just shout. We're taking it to the streets. The walls are coming down. We must build a new world on the bricks of destruction. Death to the pig$ and power brokers. Dick Nixon before he dicks us. We will prevail."

That fall, Sara took a job with the U of I English Department cataloguing the papers of distinguished graduates. Mine, she said, were not among them, "but you have plenty of time to change that."

I found myself going for lengthy walks, often disappearing for entire afternoons. I followed the bike paths that shadowed the Iowa River, roads that climbed the winding hills and infiltrated quiet neighborhoods. I began to notice things, things that didn't directly relate to my own desires and fears. I watched fall become winter, watched diamonds magically appear and disappear in the snow as I passed. I watched the waters rise in the spring. I studied the others who trespassed upon my solitude, the thinkers and brooders, the jock-strapped runners (there weren't so many then), the young couples with babies and automatic garage doors glinting in their eyes.

The ducks were always present, I recall, those all-knowing beings from another planet or plane, lords of the river, amusing me with their sounds and movements, yet all the while studying me, obviously amused by my sounds and movements. Amused by my suspicion that my actions had some meaning.

I also observed plenty of signs that Clifford Moss, like Ernest Gripp before him, had been correct. The Revolution was dead. Stillborn. I no longer encountered comrades and brothers, only students and hangers-on who were frantically searching for new diversions—and leaders.

"You won't believe what I saw on the Pentacrest green," I told Sara one evening late in the spring of '74. "Lonny X was passing out leaflets for a 'cryogenic passport to the future.' 'Leave now while your body is whole,' he said, before boasting he'd be frozen as soon as he signed up five initiates."

"But that's Lonny X," Sara responded. "You've said it yourself: he's a born follower. And in the absence of worthy leaders, what choices does he have?"

I let Sara enjoy another of her subtle victories, refusing to renew our ongoing debate, even when she added, "So maybe the question isn't, what about Lonny X? Maybe the question is, what about you? What do you believe?"

"You mean, apart from the fact that Lonny X will outlive us by several millennia?"

Sara shook her head and laughed. She, too, knew it was time to stop, before she said something like, "You've been given a lifelong grant to write, for Christ's sake. But you won't even pick up a pen. You're becoming so negative . . . about everything. What's happening to you?" And I retreated to my room on Market Street.

A pleasant, if imperfect, memory comes back to me—one of the better ones I've had since arriving in D.C. Sara and I are attempting to camp in the woods adjoining Coralville Reservoir, a few miles north of Iowa City. Moonlight airbrushes the landscape ever so gently, emphasizing only the soft and beautiful, concealing nature's imperfections. Helped by my steady intake of wine, the moon brings out a certain warmth in Sara's features. She looks good. Very good.

I know Sara has romance in mind, and the evening is moving promisingly, albeit slowly, in that direction when we begin counting and naming the stars. "31, Bud." "32, Ralph." "33, Rosie."

"You're obsessed," she laughs whenever I dub one of them "Ernest" or "Rad." We give up somewhere in the upper 120s. "Leonard. Lenny, to his planets," is as far as we progress.

"I really think you're special," Sara whispers in my ear. "You know I only want to help you find your way."

"I know," is all I can say in reply. She leans her head on my shoulder.

We stare at the now nameless stars, gasp whenever a meteor flares. Time becomes irrelevant, an outmoded concept. Unfortunately, I spoil whatever romantic mood the moon and the stars have helped create when I collapse unexpectedly into unconscious sleep, cruelly colliding with the rocks and twigs between our faltering fire and the Cub-Scout-size tent, firmly clutching my bottle of Mad Dog 20/20 throughout.

At least we wake up together the next morning. Sara has pressed her body against mine on the bumpy ground, then pulled the sleeping bag up to our necks like a blanket. The sun is just beginning to warm our faces. "How did you sleep?" she asks, at the same time retrieving a pebble from beneath her neck. "And don't say, 'Like a rock.'"

In the autumn of '74—the year in which Nixon ultimately dicked himself—the Breeze left Iowa City, quietly, as was her style. Sara had landed a near-subsistence-wage job at a textbook publishing firm in Boston. Despite my emotional turmoil, I admired her for this; she was one of the few female English majors I'd known who didn't plan to be either a grade-school teacher or a suicidal, Plathian poet.

I can see her now, staring at me with her light blue eyes. Those eyes had come to frighten me with their honesty and directness, even more so with their power to see past my bullshit. I knew Sara was waiting for me to say something—anything—to hint at the possibility of a future together.

"I'm sure we'll be together again," I said. When her expression told me these words were not achieving their intended effect, I followed them with a lie that made us both uncomfortable. "Send me some information when you get to Boston. Maybe I'll apply for a job there."

It was the best I could do.

I knew I would miss her, of course, although I couldn't have known how much or often.

But part of me—a large part of me—was coldly relieved. I was free of all responsibility, of all expectations, free from judging, caring eyes. I went for one of my longest walks that night. Deliberately lost.

CHAPTER 7

AM I THE ONLY ONE who finds it odd that a "So This Is Your First Visit to Washington" map would pinpoint the city's police stations? It certainly prompts the question, are muggings and drive-by shootings generally part of that First Visit tourist package? Or perhaps a foresighted mapmaker had anticipated my particular situation—the onetime pseudo-revolutionary called out of retirement by a pseudo-terrorist, humbly crawling to the "pig oppressor" for help.

"If you hate the police," a bumper sticker once taunted me from the back of a neighbor's car as I was speeding home from Dubuque High on a hand-me-down English Racer, "the next time you're in trouble, call a hippie."

Whatever the motives behind its drafting, the map has directed me to the station closest to Scott's Buncombese bastion, to the Special Operations Division at Washington Circle. That's how the sign above the door reads, anyway, but there's nothing special about the station itself. Its walls and ceiling are painted, uniformly, in vomit green, the DCC school color. It even has the standard-issue front desk, implying that anyone can walk in off the street with a "special operations" request. A rotund black sergeant stands behind the desk, finishing a joke. His colleagues, scattered about the dreary lobby, are laughing as they turn to face me.

"I've come to turn myself in," I say.

"Well," he roars without pausing a second, "you've come to the right place." There is a second burst of laughter, but it stops—most of it anyway, bar a few snickers—when I tell them who I am.

"Give me that again," the sergeant says. He narrows his dark brown eyes, revealing a patchwork of deeply etched crow's-feet. He's older than I first guessed, and for the first time he looks like a big-city cop, like someone who's seen too many unsolved murders, too many dead teenagers. He's not being drawn into my story; there's no "willing suspension of disbelief," as Gripp would say, only a suspension of joviality. A small crowd is gathering at the front desk. Everyone is dressed smartly in black.

"I've been following the wire reports all day," a female detective offers. "Huxley is in the hands of the FBI."

"And I've been watching CNN," a male counterpart adds. "Huxley ain't here, and you ain't Huxley."

"Let's see some ID. You must have a driver's license or Social Security card." I know what's coming. "Maybe a credit card or two."

I try to explain that when I walked away from my dying Dodge Dart in 1978, right after it carried me to Denver, I also walked away from my last identification card. My Iowa driver's license, well beyond its renewal date even then, had been one of only two I'd ever carried, the other being my much abused Selective Service registration card, torn in half, taped together, singed by flame on all four corners.

"I don't believe in reducing a person's identity to ten or twelve digits on a plastic card," I declare. "If you want to pledge allegiance to some corporate executive's idea of a brave new world, that's your choice. But I refuse to carry a passport." This is news to me as well; in truth I never gave ID cards much thought before my unexpected coming out. Denver's book- and record-store employees had never ex-hibited an unwillingness to accept my twenty-dollar bills. No register runners at Wax Trax or the Tattered Cover really cared who I was or where I lived, as long as they collected the money due.

Actually, only one person had complained, consistently if indirectly, about my lack of IDs. Twice each month for the past two decades, my father had sent me a fresh stack of those same twenty-dollar bills by certified, registered, insured-to-the-maximum-allowable-amount mail. And each time he did so, he enclosed a familiar admonishment: "A checking account would make this so much simpler."

"That's pretty damned convenient," a young skeptic, leaning against the front desk, comments. "Without an ID, you can be anyone you want to be."

A voice from the back room casts the deciding vote for disbelief. "I've got the Bureau on the line. They've still got Huxley."

"No, they don't," I say, "and they're not going to have me, either. The FBI talks too much. I want *you* to take me to the Burger King. This is your city, isn't it?"

The sergeant looks me up and down. "Thanks for giving yourself up peacefully and sparing us any unnecessary bloodshed," he says, again to the amusement of his fellow officers. "But next time, do us a favor and try to be someone we haven't already caught, like D. B. Cooper or something. I don't know if you heard my friend back there, but the governor has granted you a pardon. So run along now, and let us get some work done."

The voice in the back has an additional suggestion for me as I exit. "If you want to be on the news, go to a TV station, not a police station." Angered and offended, I let the door slam behind me, as if to say, "Next time, I will call a hippie." But my anger doesn't keep me from realizing the accidental truth of the anonymous heckler's advice.

On a corner near the police station, I see something I've never seen before: the militant pedestrian. While making a wide left turn, a flower delivery van veers too close to a young businesswoman in the crosswalk, and she responds by swatting the van's hollow metal side with her hand. The sound this makes, a boomeranging thud, surprises me almost as much as it does the driver. An instant later, he is standing beside his vehicle, ready to hurl a few choice expletives at the pedestrian. But he ends up directing them at the truck instead. His van is still in drive, and it is slowly moving away from him—twenty feet, thirty feet, fifty and gaining speed—stopping only when it collides head-on with a full-size Metro bus in the opposite lane, making an even more surprising sound. The woman laughs and briskly walks away, as do her fellow travelers.

Back in Lafayette Park, CBS reporter Helen Toxberry is filing a story on "day two of the hostage situation." I've seen her reports on the four o'clock *First News* program produced by Denver's CBS affiliate. It's the only "news" program I've watched where viewers are offered cash prizes over the phone. In one more attempt to bring newscasting down to the level of Lowest Common Denominator, members of the audience are asked to repeat the names of shows from the network's dismal prime-time fare, all of which, I'm sure, are LCD-approved.

Helen's having trouble taping her report, because every protester in the world seems to have come to the city to take advantage of its bloated media presence, and the disparate groups are jockeying for the camera space behind Toxberry. The Love Earth First Team has secured a prominent position in the lineup, with their "Global warming burns me up" signs. Next to them are the razor-scalped representatives of the National Association for the Advancement of White Pinheads. Their heads look like dented cue balls; their signs advise, "Send the niggers back to Africa."

"We were here first," the Native American Guard counters. "Send the Caucasians back to Europe."

The Friendly Enemies of War hoist graphic depictions of a mushroom cloud, highlighted with the caption "Your tax dollars at work."

There are other signs as well. "Death to Capital Punishment." "Abort Abortionists." "Rabbits get sprayed in their eyes. Torture someone your own size."

The various contingents are all shouting their slogans, too, drowning Toxberry's attempts beneath their waves of zeal, some capped with hysteria, even as she increases the volume of her voice with each word. I take my cue and dive into the froth. "Excuse me," I announce, "but this is very important. I'm Rod Huxley. I'm the person wanted at the Burger King."

"Cut," Toxberry yells.

I tell her again who I am, then begin to ask if she can arrange a rendezvous with the terrorist.

"Out of my way, you goddamn creep, I've dealt with enough kooks today. Larry, get him outta here!"

Her bulky, broad-shouldered assistant gently sets down his camera and lifts me, not so gently, in its stead. I land, again not so gently, in the middle of the howling protesters. "Get out of here, you pig," an antiwar storm trooper spits in my ear. "You're detracting from our legitimacy."

"Are you all asleep? I am Rod Huxley, the source of your speculative blabbering—"

"Give me back the goddamn microphone," Toxberry commands. "Larry! How could you have let this moron back on our shoot?"

Toxberry's tugging at my sleeve as I explain, "The FBI has screwed everything up, and the police don't even want to know what's going on. You've got to help me get into the Burger King. I'm running out of time. We all are. Why can't you understand?"

Apart from one woman erupting "There's no zone like Ozone," the protesters are uniformly silent. They stare at my face, more than a little perplexed—and completely jealous of the attention I'm receiving.

"Larry! Quit messing with your goddamn camera and help me out over here. Larry!"

Minutes later, I am standing in a second police station, facing a second desk sergeant. Unlike the first, he is pale and thin, a walking corpse of a man, and true to that image, he lacks the vital signs that would indicate the presence of humor.

"You really don't have an ID?" He scowls but doesn't wait for an answer before turning to the arresting officer. "What do we book him for? Creating a public disturbance isn't much of a reason to hold him."

"We could book him for assault, but he looked like the one being assaulted. Old Toxinberry was really laying into him. She didn't need any help, but she was getting plenty of it from her cameraman. Maybe there's some FCC rule about interfering with the responsible broadcasting of news. He had their microphone."

"Naw, then we'd have to arrest everyone in television news," gripes the sergeant. "You don't want Sam Donaldson here any more than I do, and the ACLU would be on us in a second. Tell you what. How about we give him a phone call and a few hours to decompress?"

They both look at me with a frustration bordering on weariness, then turn to face each other, as if silently sharing a question, "Remember when we dealt with criminals instead of lunatics?"

"So what's in the bag?" the desk sergeant asks.

"Nothing much," his minion replies. "An old razor. A pair of even older underwear. Some letters he's been carrying around since high school."

"Let me see." The sergeant slowly removes one of the letters from my Safeway grocery sack, then examines it with painstaking care. "So are you Aaron Scott?"

"No, that's what I've been trying to tell you. Those letters were written to me. I'm the guy wanted in the Burger King. You should be taking me there. Now. You'll get your names in the paper, I promise."

"Written to you, huh? That would make you 'Mr. Komrade,' with a K. Wouldn't that be correct?" He places the letter back in the sack, along with the others, including one that actually includes a "Dear Rod" salutation, the one mailed from Boston to Iowa City almost twenty-one years ago.

"You've got a phone call coming," the other cop grudgingly informs me.

Needless to say, it is with much regret that I dial the FBI's main number. "This is Rod Huxley, most wanted of the most wanted. May I speak to the person in charge." After a pause of two minutes, I hear at least four phones picking up on the other end of the line.

"I want to walk into the Burger King alone," I tell an Agent Farmingdale. "Obviously, the terrorist has some things he wants to discuss with me. I doubt that he wants an audience." After a long conversation, made that way by the grating gaps of silence and white noise that follow my every remark, I am told to "hold tight."

"Don't go anywhere."

I am taken to a holding cell and placed on exhibition for the officers who are supposed to be working. Only two of them are present, and they are in the middle of a late-afternoon meal. With Big Macs sitting on each of their desks, I am tempted to tell them how hungry I am, then ask if they'd consider a second McDonalds run.

"Did you hear the president on TV this morning?" one of them loudly inquires of the other. "'We must stay calm and exercise caution.' What kind of candyass response is that? I mean, who's in that Burger King? Saddam Hussein? I say, blow the damn place up. No one will miss a few tourists. I sure as hell won't."

"That's no lie. You ever get behind 'em on the subway escalators? How hard is it to stand to the right so other people can pass? I always make a point of trying to bowl 'em over."

"They might as well shoot that Hucklebee guy, too," contends the more vociferous of the two. "In fact, I'll bet you that's exactly what happens. I mean, come on, you're going to have hundreds of guns trained on that wacko and his terrorist, and you want to tell me no one's going to fire? Hell, I wouldn't mind being on the line myself when the shooting starts. I could handle that assignment. I'd pull the trigger in a second. You've got to admit, it would sure beat the shit out of shoveling paper all day."

They can cancel the McDonalds run. For one of the few times in my life that I can recall, my appetite has deserted me.

"You know what I think? I think the terrorist and Hucklebee are in it together. That's right. He's probably one of Hucklebee's old commie bosses. And now that there's no room for them in Russia, he's come here to cause trouble."

Their spirited discussion is interrupted by an even livelier one at the front desk, out of my sight. "But we *are* taking him," someone is insisting. "He's ours."

Three men in suits are coming my way, and there, framed by a pair of more expensively dressed colleagues, is Special Agent Fenwick. He looks at his wristwatch, then looks up at me. "What exactly do you take me for?" he asks as he approaches the cell. "You didn't think you and I were finished?"

CHAPTER 8

"SAY, DIDN'T YOU HAVE A BEARD?" asks Fenwick, astute as ever. We are nearing an architectural horror named after the anti-democratic defender of American democracy, J. Edgar Hoover. Approaching a tunnel entrance, we pass a concrete-coated courtyard, and standing within it are dozens of tourists waiting to begin what must be an official, propaganda-laden look at select sites in the building. I'm sure they won't be seeing any of Hoover's prizes: the computers loaded with megabytes of data about insignificant people like me, or the older, yellowing files on official Bureau procedures for blackmailing presidents and civil rights leaders.

In an underground parking area, we exit the car. Fenwick flashes his badge to a security guard at an X-ray station, then takes me up an elevator and into a maze of dark, sharply twisting corridors. I expect to see a large piece of cheese at any turn. But what I get to see is how the FBI actually works.

"I'm sorry if I made your job difficult," I say as we make another corner.

"It's okay," Fenwick tells me. "The story here is I deliberately let you go so I could tail you. That way, if you were involved in a conspiracy, you would have led me to the others. Just don't say anything to mess me up when you meet my boss. I would like to keep my job."

We've come to the end of a hallway. Fenwick opens a glass door for me.

"We're so pleased you've decided to trust us, Mr. Huxley. This is good, because we're looking at a very dangerous situation. You will need our full cooperation, just as we will need yours." The person telling me this is Fenwick's boss, a surprisingly young, surprisingly attractive woman. She reads *Washingtonian, Architectural Digest,* and *Congressional Quarterly*—at least that's the impression she wants to give from the carefully arranged display on the black, leather-accented table in her office. Her name tag reads, unapologetically, "*Ms.* Foster," and she is draped in fairly bright colors for an employee of the Federal Bureau of Investigation, or even a resident of Washington, D.C. I look at her feet to see if she's wearing the notorious black, shiny FBI shoes. Not only are her feet out of uniform, I find, but her legs are well formed, just a few aerobics classes away from a beer commercial's image of perfection.

"We've secured a hotel room for the night for you and Fenwick," she says, batting a loose strand of blond hair away from her face. "You're facing a busy day tomorrow, and Special Agent Fenwick will be able to prepare you. Then, you're going to get a good night's sleep while we give your terrorist one more chance to slip into dreamland and make this a lot easier for all of us. Already, we're talking at least forty-six hours without sleep. If that doesn't happen, you'll still have the advantage of being well rested."

When Fenwick learns that the room is at the Best Western Midtown, his sigh is audible.

"It was the best we could do," Department Head Foster says, now with a steely, authoritative sternness in her once-lilting voice. "The press has taken over all the good hotels—at least all the ones up to your impeccable standards."

"You may be in for more than a busy day tomorrow," Fenwick informs me once he and I have taken over Room 1206. "Your terrorist has a briefcase crammed full of explosives. There's no way out for this lunatic, I'm afraid. Once you're in there, that Burger King might just go up in a ball of flame."

He pauses and lets his mouth relax into a slight smile. "'Charbroiled,' isn't that their claim to fame?"

He then tells me, "I've got something I need to show you," and pulls three pieces of paper from his well-worn, explosive-free briefcase. Fenwick hands me what turns out to be an internal FBI memo.

"This will be tomorrow's lead story in the liberal press," he confides. "Dan Rather doesn't even know it exists yet. You're seeing it first."

"You want to brand bar codes onto the wrists of American citizens?"

"Wrong memo," he says, snatching the top sheet from my hands. "Do me a favor and pretend you never saw that, even though it is an idea whose time has come. Here, read the other one, the two-pager."

"Early this morning, suspect freed elderly hostage complaining of diabetes," the memo begins. "A grateful grandmother of sixteen, she reports young man had treated them well. Fed them well, too, although she is sick of cheeseburgers and fries." Buried in the dense memorandum are several conjectures and facts I don't think the press will be seeing, like "Situation deemed extremely dangerous" and "President wants damage confined to two-block area."

Worse yet, there's a frightening passage about ordering "psychological probes" and "expansive memory serum tests" for the terrorist's elderly victim—apparently, like me, still a hostage. At the very bottom of page two, almost as a postscript, the author of this internal report finally remembers to include the day's biggest bombshell, obtained courtesy of the FBI's grandmother.

"One more thing, according to victim: the young man is a woman."

Fenwick, not surprisingly, is eager to talk.

"A woman terrorist. Did you see that? I can't believe this has all been for some mixed-up babe. You got some outstanding paternity suit or something?"

Fenwick waits for my nonforthcoming laugh, and when he doesn't hear it, probably thinks he's stumbled onto the truth. "I'm sure you're all for women's lib," he says, sounding as dated as my book. "'Burn the bra' and all that claptrap. That's one revolution that succeeded, unfortunately—women getting jobs, women gaining power. They're too emotional, too unpredictable. Maybe it just figures that the terrorist is a woman."

"Every morning I eat my Frosted Flakes," I say, "and I read the paper to acquaint myself with the latest murderers and sadists, or to see who's started the latest war. It hasn't come to my attention that men have given up their hold on those prized jobs. I'm sure women will get their turn eventually, and I'm sure they'll do fine when given the chance. They probably are too emotional. After all, they evolved from the same apes we did. Personally, I've always thought cats should rule the world. But as long as *homo sapiens* retains its brutal monopoly, I'm certain the untested female majority couldn't be any worse at running things than men have been."

"You never worked for a woman," Fenwick replies. "Sorry, I forgot. You never worked, period. My boss is a mean broad. You saw her. She treats me like I'm some kind of idiot, never mind that I've been doing this twenty years longer than she has. I mean, did you hear her? 'Don't let him out of your sight.' Like I'm gonna let you walk away again. You want to tell me she didn't get her job from some quotafied system of reverse discrimination? She reminds me of that nutty broad who got me in trouble at Berkeley. All work and no play." He adds, "If *Miss* Foster knew you'd disappeared that first time without my knowing, she'd have my ass in a sling. She'd have my nuts, which is what those women libbers are really after, anyway."

"She seemed fairly impressive to me," I tell him. "I can't say I've ever yearned for a boss, but if I absolutely had to have one, I think I'd settle for an attractive, intelligent woman. Fenwick, you're fighting the march of history. You should learn to live with it, accept it, maybe even enjoy it. You might find that women aren't so bad."

"Is that why you're single?" Fenwick asks. "Oh, I get it. You only like women in theory. Or would that apply to people in general?"

After Fenwick talks himself to sleep, his snoring signals me that it is safe to leave the room. I'm wide awake myself, having downed three Diet Pepsis to counter the sedative powers of his talk, the verbal exhaust that filled Room 1206 like Denver smog, irritating my mind with cancerous theories on everything from fetal rights to the incorrectness of political correctness. I swipe the room key from the dresser top, grab my jacket, and slip silently, like a panther, into the night.

Well, almost. An agent is standing in the hallway, guarding our door. "Fenwick asked me to grab some more pop," I say.

"Pop?"

"Umm, Pepsi. Coke."

"Oh, soda," he says. "I'm surprised he didn't ask me to handle the matter."

"He would have," I tell the young, neatly groomed man, "but I needed to stretch my legs. I'll be right back. Fenwick's probably already getting impatient."

"Oh. Yes, sir." He steps aside and watches me pass.

Where the Washington day has been unseasonably warm, the night conforms more closely to my idea of October. My jacket no longer feels heavy. It is unable to shield me from the humid chill. The hookers near the hotel bare testament to the positive effects of heroin addiction, their forced smiles oblivious to the cold, their short dresses not quite covering their goose-pimpled butts. Are these the positions of power Fenwick derided? The fruits of successful revolution? Perhaps this is what Marx meant in that insulting, mystifying reference to a "community of women" in his *Manifesto.*

Heading south on Fourteenth Street, I discover another nocturnal creature, the Washington Monument, now strangely alive, its shape silhouetted by a circle of spotlights. Two eerie red eyes glare from each of the four faces of its pointy top—or so I assume, since I can see only two—apparently to terrify pilots who have steered their planes into restricted airspace. These rudimentary eyes have transmuted the monument into a primeval worm defiantly hoisting its unsegmented invertebrate body from the sea's primordial slime.

It is with this image filling my eyes that I think of the brief speech I'd been saving for Aaron Hamilton Scott III, the speech I would never give, to the terrorist who never was.

"The revolution's over. We were the victors. We were the losers. Now we are anachronisms. Let's go home."

He would then let me and the other hostages go, letting go, in the process, of our shackled-together pasts. Or he would defiantly blow a Burger King to the heavens, in ironic imitation of the war-plotting society he thought he abhorred.

I think of the women I have known and wonder who is sitting only a few city blocks from here, fending off sleep with caffeine and fear. Could it be someone from Dubuque High, say, Twila Thorne, the red-haired "fox" who relieved me of my virginity, then dumped me for a Camaro and the greaseball who drove it? Given the life she's probably led since trading me in, she may have come to appreciate the one man in America who refuses to own a car. Or perhaps it's Regina Mae, chair of the twentieth reunion, still angered by the fact that their one quasi-celebrity had not attended, that he couldn't be bothered to see who had turned into accountants, car dealers, teachers, and the like, that he'd returned the request for information with a curt "Killed in Vietnam."

And what about Sara? Of everyone who's coming to mind, she would probably be my first choice, were I being given one. Yet I can't imagine her doing something so irrational and dangerous to others. Not the Sara I knew.

More likely it's a vengeful Megan Reilly, returning to remind me that love and romance are not part of my dharma, that they were meant only to bring me pain and humiliation. Meg helped poison the very last of my ideals, which had already withered like neglected houseplants. Has she come here now to make sure none have grown back?

I wonder if this isn't a mystery worth preserving—something to ponder on the long train ride home. Union Station's not far from here. I could start walking now.

A few minutes later, however, I'm back in the hallway outside our hotel room. "Jesus." Fenwick's subordinate appears to be on the verge of crying. "Where did you go? I peeked inside and the Special Agent was sleeping. It's been over an hour. You coulda cost me my job."

"Sorry," I say, "but the soda machines in this building don't take twenties."

Everything changes. This, to paraphrase the dead Greek Heraclitus, is the only certainty. Tomorrow the Washington Monument will have reverted to its previous form, the benign obelisk, loved by tourists, envied by sex therapists. I will awake an exile in a strange and dangerous land, deserted even by Aaron Hamilton Scott III.

CHAPTER 9

CATS ARE THE ONLY REMINDERS of my second brush with serious commitment. This lasted through most of 1978, in an apartment on a hill overlooking the Iowa River. Meg said she loved kittens, so we bought two. But apart from giving them names on the drive home from Iowa City's new supermall, she mostly ignored them. I cared for Wagner and Brahms, kept their water dishes full and their litter box clean, and the three of us fell in love.

Meg worked as an assistant classical guitar instructor. Naively I'd thought, "Artist-artist. This could be good for me." Maybe she'd inspire me to do something. Anything.

I met her at a Friends of Old-Time Music concert. An ancient white man had sauntered onto the stage at Hatcher Auditorium, where he proceeded to pluck an equally ancient banjo.

"I'd be glad to give you mine" had been Meg's first words to me when I entered the lobby sometime after the performance had ended, clutching the musician's barely legible autograph. "It's probably worth more, even now."

I found her words somewhat cold and jarring, but she did inject humor into her critique of the banjoist's technique as we walked from Hatcher to the Yellow Line bus stop. Her sparkling hazel eyes and beguiling smile confused me as well; they seemed at odds with her words, made me think the harshness was simply a front for a gentler, more sensitive soul (she was a musician, after all). So by the time she asked, "Did you notice how bony he was?" her smile was all I could see—that and the way her shoulder-length auburn hair shimmered each time we passed a streetlight.

"I'm serious," she laughed. "He couldn't have weighed more than 100 pounds. I thought he was going to fall over under the weight of his banjo." The words were secondary, as light and empty of meaning as the clouds of steam they formed in the cold night air.

Our bus ride lasted only seconds, such is the power of relativity. Each time Meg smiled, she made me think of every bittersweet love song I had listened to on headphones in my room in Father's house, of every yearning "I know she's out there somewhere" ballad. I should have recognized her smile for what it was, the craftsmanship of a very expensive orthodontist. "You're *that* Rod Huxley?" she said, again displaying those perfect teeth. "You must have some very interesting stories. I'd love to hear them."

During our first weeks together, Meg was quick to laugh. She was kind, self-effacing, even motivating at times. When Meg first stayed over at my place, we were children exploring new neighborhoods, cheerful, carefree, and most of all, curious. She didn't make me feel I should apologize for anything I had or had not done.

In the months after I moved in with her, she became the most moody, hypercritical, uninspiring being imaginable. Although she liked my Beatles and Bob Marley records, she didn't even pretend to tolerate my import 45s by The Clash or Sex Pistols. "If these people aren't capable of producing a melody with more than three notes, then they are not composers, they are poets," she said. "And then, frankly, I much prefer Longfellow or Keats."

Meg called me the "retired writer," and sometimes, the "revolutionary in exile."

"Where do you go on your walks?" she would ask, letting me glimpse her jealousy at the rewards of my mystery achievement. "It must be nice never having to wake up to a Monday morning" was another of her stock comments. Though this may have been true, the words seemed oddly out of place in her mouth, as her schedule of lessons, classes, and recitals had little in common with the traditional work week.

"One day something will happen," Meg chided me. "Your money will run out, along with your damned blind luck, and your long weekend will be over. You'll be waking up like the rest of us."

"You know what I think?" she started in on me another evening. "I think you're the jealous one. You resent everyone, because other people actually do things, without thinking them into the dirt. They haven't turned procrastination into a way of life. That's why you're so critical of people like your brother in Omaha."

Why did I put up with it? I was an idiot, albeit a commonplace one. While our arguments may have been tedious and winner-free, our sex was good, especially compared with not having any for months at a time. Meg, it was hard not to notice, looked great from any angle, and I became familiar with several of those angles.

And she wasn't always negative. Inexplicably, Meg's smile returned whenever I talked about my "revolutionary past," something I did only at her urging. On the occasions she sat down to eat a meal with me, Meg would offer loving glances in exchange for the finer details of that experience. "Did Sara help write the essays?" "So who exactly was this Lazlo Rope?" Reluctantly, I answered these questions, mystified as to why she found this one isolated part of my life so interesting.

"How come you're so fascinated by the bee-in?" I would say, and Meg would reply, "I'm fascinated by *you*." Then she would ask about Ernest Gripp and my television appearance.

Meg's hobbies—jogging and cocaine—reminded me that times had changed. I actually tried running with her once along the rim of the Coralville Reservoir. The sun was generous with its warmth, the breeze softly soothing. It could have been a perfect afternoon had it been put to better use. As it was, sweat glued my faded, one-size-too-small "George Jackson Died for Your Sins" T-shirt to my stomach and back, salt stung my eyes, and Meg turned my efforts into a cliché by—literally—running circles around me. I tried to double my pace and escape, but the circle remained unbroken, and I succeeded only in doubling the pain in my heart and lungs.

"Come on, Trotsky," Meg called out, using another of her pet insults. "You've got to outrun the tide of history. You don't want to end up with a pickax in your skull."

When Meg finally said, "Forget this. I'll meet you at the car in an hour," I decided to give up on attaining physical fitness in one afternoon and simply hobbled back to the lot, a good fifty yards from where we had started.

Two thirds of the way, I stopped to rest in a crowded picnic area and felt every muscle in my body contracting as I struggled to lower myself onto the bench of the only table not in use. "What the hell does she see in me?" I wondered, wiping my face with the front of my T-shirt. "Why does she stay? Why do I stay?"

"Daddy, look at that man," a small girl interrupted these thoughts. "He makes funny noises like Grandma."

Back at Meg's apartment, I could barely extract my swollen feet from my stiff, steel-toed boots. "I told you you needed running shoes," she scolded me predictably. "You know, maybe you should try working out on your own. That way you could build up gradually to my level."

I'm not sure I can explain my aversion to the coke; I had, after all, tried every controlled substance short of heroin. I think my distaste for the drug had something to do with the attitude that accompanied it, with my observation that co-caine was used by the same people who used that dreaded new word, "lifestyle." Maybe it was latent sixties snobbishness on my part, but I had a bias toward educational drugs—LSD and the like—as opposed to recreational drugs. "Tuning in," I remembered hearing from one of my generation's self-certified gurus, was as important as "turning on." But all coke did was make me want to talk all night, without giving me anything to say. Oddly, however, Meg didn't try to stop me when this happened. Rather, she propped me up with ques-tions. "Tell me more about Rad Brad. Did you two ever rec-oncile your differences?" "How did you feel when you learned about the bee-in's failure?"

Meg smoked a lot of pot as well, the one drug lost in the smoke-gray area between educational and recreational. But soon I was smoking my last. Once an undemanding friend, marijuana now wanted something in return for its formerly unselfish revelations. Even a few hits made me think too much, strapping me onto a roller coaster of dizzying doubts. It made me remember. "I think pleasure has stopped giving me plea-sure," I told Meg on the last of those rising, plummeting, wish-I-had-a-seat-belt nights.

"So you're becoming a straight," she sneered, back in her usual negative mode. "Big surprise." I turned on the televi-sion, a reflex that was fast becoming a habit for both of us, even during the hours we once set aside for the only thing we did well as a couple.

My walks became even longer. On most days, I bought my lunch at the university's Memorial Union, then took it outside. I stared at the coeds sunbathing by the river, heard them giggle and talk about their dates. I imagined them to be outgoing and uncomplicated, free of false expectations, anx-ious, perhaps, to meet a onetime fourth-rate celebrity. Most of all, I imagined them naked.

Late that October, I received a letter from my brother. "I just wanted to let you know I'm sorry about our falling out," he wrote. "Maybe we'll see each other this Christmas." Tyler enclosed an unrelated clipping from *People* magazine. In an article that set out to determine "Where Are They Now?" wannabe-world-savior Rod Huxley was dismissed in two vitriolic sentences: "He's disappeared . . . and no one cares. Perhaps he's cooking up a comeback, but will anyone be interested in his leftovers?"

"That's interesting," Meg said, looking over my shoulder. "Can I see it when you're through?"

Before I could answer, our cats charged out of the bedroom and into the kitchen, Wagner chasing Brahms. They galloped across the wooden floors like tiny stallions on a dusty plain. "I don't see what's so remarkable about it," I said at last, "but be my guest. Frame it and hang it on the wall, for all I care."

Sara's letter, mailed from Boston and forwarded from my first Iowa City address, surprised me even more. "Greetings from the real world," it began.

> You have no idea what it's like out here. I thought the field of educational publishing would be exempt, but there's so much bullshit, both personal and political, to deal with. I can smell it the minute I come in from the street where the trolley lets me off. I think it seeps in through the ventilation system. I know it's not coming in through the open windows, because there aren't any in this building.
>
> My boss is a real classic. He's in his mid thirties, thinks he's in his early twenties, looks like he's in his late forties. His hairline is retreating faster than a glacier at the end of an ice age. His skin is a faint, sickly yellow because he drinks gallons of carrot juice and pops Vitamin C, all to make up for the fact that he's never been outside on a sunny day. It's pretty pathetic.

When I was new here, my co-workers dragged me to what they called a "singles bar." It was my first and last time. But anyway, there he was, the Man Who Would Be Boss, Mr. Dennis Dill. He was right in his element, hanging out at the bar with the other creeps, ready to go home with anything on two legs. As for my own impressions of the place, I was fearing the outbreak of fire, noting that two polyester suits might brush against one another. At least no one got around to asking me, "Your condo or mine?"

Each morning Dill comes in an hour after the rest of us. He's always in a bad mood, and it's always the result of a hangover from the night before. He mellows out a bit after his lunch, for reasons you can easily guess. But sometimes after he returns, he forgets he's still at work and not in one of his bars. He comes on to me and most of the other women working in this department. Sometimes he's subtle. Most of the time he's not. Like when he asked me if I'd ever "done it" with an older, experienced man. I should have retorted, "Done what? The laundry? Heroin?" Worse yet was the time he said, "I know you find me attractive." I set him straight, only to have him come back with, "Well, maybe you could find me attractive for half an hour." I wanted to barf but laughed it off. I told him he had a great sense of humor. That's probably the only recourse I really have. He is my boss, after all. I have to deal with the jerk. I need the paycheck.

Unfortunately, the job itself is somewhat harder to laugh off. Still, I may finally have a way to make it more interesting. It's too much to explain in a letter, but let's just say I gave myself a promotion. A few added responsibilities here and there, unbeknownst to Dill. It's probably the only advancement I'll see here. You have no idea how lucky you are to have been spared this. Why don't you write a *Cookbook for Survival* for me and everyone else out here in the trenches? I could do the research, seeing as I'm already doing it every day. There's a book just waiting to be written. If I had the time, I'd be doing it myself. Plus, Dill has been so critical of everything I've written as an editor. It hasn't done much for my confidence.

There's so much more I could tell you, and I think you'd find my stories of life in the real world of interest. There's a toll-free number at work. Why don't you give me a call?

Two weeks passed. I walked another few hundred miles without actually going anywhere and withstood one more bruising, inconclusive argument with Meg before I summoned the energy to dial Sara's number.

"Miss Caine is no longer in our employ," a shrill, recording-like voice assaulted me.

"You must be mistaken," I replied. "A great deal of thought and effort went into making this call. Could you please check your directory again? She works in the Production Editorial Department."

"I assure you I am not mistaken. Miss Caine's dismissal was no small matter here. Perhaps you'd care to speak with someone in Personnel, or I could put you through to her superior, Mr. Dill."

"I would be happy to speak with a 'superior' of Sara Caine, but I doubt that you have any 'in your employ.' Perhaps you could give me a home telephone number for her instead?"

"I'm sorry, but we do not have Miss Caine's home telephone number, and if we did, I would not be at liberty to reveal it. Thank you for calling Winston-Bailey."

I sat alone in Meg's apartment that evening. Meg was out tutoring one of her many "hopeless cases," the ones from whom she demanded payment in advance. I was staring down a hopeless case of my own, a blank piece of typing paper. The sheet of paper ultimately won. It steadfastly refused to transform itself into a letter.

One afternoon in December, I returned from a walk to hear Meg playing her guitar. She was picking two notes, rapidly, back and forth. "What's that you're playing?" I asked as I approached her work area, the old throw rug off her side of the bed. She used the hardwood floor as her desktop. There was paper all around her.

"Just something I'm working on." She stopped her picking. "It's for my master's."

"No, I mean that two-note thing," I said.

"It's called a trill. G and F-sharp." She demonstrated it for me.

"It sounds like bees," I said.

"That's good," she replied. "It's supposed to."

"But I don't like *bees*," I reminded her of the obvious. "I can't stand the thought of them. Why are you doing this?"

"I'm sorry. I was through for today anyway." As she spoke, she reached to her right to straighten a stack of music manuscript paper.

"Is this all part of your project?" I asked.

"Oh, um, no. It's nothing."

"So let me hear some of it," I said, kneeling down beside her. "Wait a minute, what's this?" I snatched a sheet of typing paper that stuck out from the pile. "'Sara's Song' . . . interesting. 'They thought they would be freein'/Folks from sea to shining sea 'n/So they planned a bee-in/But our Rodney took to fleein'.'"

"I'm going to change that second line," Meg said. "What do you think of 'The worker and plebeian'? Or 'Every oppressed human bein''? I know. Too close to 'bee-in.' It still needs some work."

"The second line? Who cares about the second line? What the fuck are you writing?"

"If you must know, I'm working on an oratorio. I wanted to surprise you. It's about a failed revolutionary and the ghosts that haunt him. But it's not about you. I swear. You're just looking at rough notes. I'm not anywhere near completing the libretto yet. Your name, for example. That's just a filler until I come up with names for my characters."

"Jesus Christ, how stupid do you think I am? You've been exploiting me for your research. That's all this has been about from the very beginning. You've been using me."

"Oh, that's rich. *You* accusing *me* of using someone. Mr. crawl-into-your-shell-whenever-life-becomes-too-complicated. Open your eyes, Rod. Look at me. Have you ever asked me how I feel about this so-called relationship? Sometimes I think you wish I would literally disappear whenever my existence is too inconvenient for you. It's like I should apologize for simply being. This is how you pushed your precious Sara away. It's how you push everyone away. Has anyone ever told you you'd make a damn good hermit?"

I could feel my anger rising. "That's bullshit and you know it. You're the one who's incapable of tolerating someone else's presence. You're the one who's been using me, remember? And by the way, isn't an oratorio supposed to be religious in theme?"

"Oh, okay," she said. "I'll rhyme 'Rod' with 'God.'"

The following morning, Wagner, Brahms, and I sneaked out while Meg was teaching a guitar class. The cats were mine now.

I'd placed a note, two lines long, between the grime-coated pans on her kitchen counter. "I used to confuse love and love songs," it read. "Thanks for the music lesson."

Wagner and Brahms cried like human infants from their Pet Taxi cages on the passenger seat of my Dodge Dart. I could have done the same, but restrained myself by calling up five bad memories for every pleasant one that intruded into my thoughts. A claustrophobic's nightmare loomed in the rearview mirror: the uneven wall of cardboard boxes, rescued from the dumpster at a state liquor store, now bulged with every record, book, and piece of clothing I owned. Hidden behind them on the back window ledge were my three shoe-box files.

"I can't believe Meg thinks I have the qualifications to become a hermit," I told my cats. "She's the one with personality problems. You've both witnessed that. We are going west to someplace new, someplace populated by people and cats who do not know us. Then we will make new friends who don't think of me as 'the guy who wrote that stupid book.' I'm not exactly sure where this place might be, but I figure if we can make it through Omaha without bumping into my brother, we should be safe."

Des Moines . . . Atlantic . . . Red Oak. I was determined to at least rid myself of Iowa on that first day of driving, even though it didn't appear anxious to go away. The exit signs weren't exactly racing by, as my Dart was refusing to live up to its name and exceed fifty miles per hour. Every semi driver reminded me of the irony in this shortcoming. They taunted me by cutting sharply into my lane before they had completely finished passing, causing me to slam the brake pedal to the floor, which in turn produced a grating, crunching blast of sound, the car's equivalent of a scream, as the brake shoes tore away what was left of their linings.

"Omaha 50 Miles," a sign finally assured me. We could be there in an hour.

As we crossed the bridge that marked the beginning of Nebraska, I considered plodding on to Lincoln, a college town similar in size to Iowa City, only an hour beyond Omaha. But the unmusical wailing of Wagner and Brahms had not improved with familiarity, nor had its volume diminished as the miles accumulated.

Confronted with a choice between stabbing my eardrums with the sharp pencil in my glove box—which was inaccessible anyway, with two cages wedged against its door—or finding a motel, I conceded it was time to conclude the feline symphony. We stopped in Omaha for the night.

Keeping my word to the cats, I did not phone my brother.

Ultimately, Denver presented itself as a likely destination. As we neared the city's eastern suburbs, I was taken in by a scene that coupled together man's aspirations and limitations. Denver's skyline, which might have looked impressive in any other geographic location, seemed puny, insignificant, dwarfed as it was by the majestic Rocky Mountains. I had found my home . . . a suspicion seconded by the glowing dash lights that warned "Oil," "Engine," and "Temperature."

Where East Colfax neared the State Capitol, I parked my car, cracked its windows, and went for a trial walk. The third Apartment for Rent sign I saw was augmented by a Pets Welcome sign. After speaking with the intoxicated manager of the Arapahoe Towers—which towered all of five stories—and unburdening myself of fifteen twenty-dollar bills, I moved my car to the loading zone in front of the building, then lugged Wagner and Brahms up five flights of stairs to explore their new home. At least the manager had been honest enough to warn me the freight elevator was out of order, even if he had forgotten to add, "Permanently."

The following morning, I found three parking tickets on the windshield of the Dart, so I drove it to the Capitol parking lot and left the keys in the ignition, along with a note on the dash that read, "You found it, you keep it."

For someone with nothing that needed to be done, I kept myself remarkably busy, at first to counter the dry, hangover-like emptiness that occasionally threatened to swallow me, symptoms of withdrawal from my dependence upon Meg Reilly. I explored much of the city on foot, getting to know its book- and record stores. I learned where Cherry Creek emptied into the South Platte River and where many of the finer fast-food restaurants were located.

Come evening, I read the opening chapters of nonfiction paperbacks, about everything and nothing, purchased from those same new- and used-book stores. I also skimmed newspapers from every part of the country, trying to understand why my lemminglike contemporaries were suddenly determined to elect a president who reminded them of their nice but goofy California uncle, who spoke of winnable nuclear wars and promised to abolish trade unions and taxes on the rich, then reintroduce the toiling masses to the subsistence wage. My reaction bordered on outrage, even genuine disbelief. I nearly registered to vote.

It wouldn't have mattered. Like an unwelcome guest with a dozen bags, the eighties had arrived. A psychotic with a handgun made certain that Lennon and McCartney would never again collaborate. Grenada fell on the eve of invading Florida. Reagan conceded the need for unions, so long as they were in Poland.

I kept walking.

On one of my expeditions—and one of my many stops at the Tattered Cover bookstore—I made the mistake of asking, "Do you stock something called *Cookbook for Revolution?*"

"We do a lot of volume here," the special assistant told me. "You bet. If a book is out of print, as this one seems to have been for some time, chances are we've sold our last copy. Let's see, *Cookbook for Newlyweds, Cookbook for Bachelors*—that's a fairly popular title. No, I don't see *Cookbook for Revolutionaries*. You know, cookbooks come and go. They're more of a seasonal thing. If it's really thirteen years old, you probably won't even find it in a used-book shop. Maybe you should try the library."

"It was a very popular book at one time," I enlightened the special assistant.

"Times change," she replied.

"I'm learning that."

My father still phoned during the first hours of daylight, when long-distance rates are at their lowest, with messages about my brother or people he thought I might have known at DCC or Dubuque High. Usually, the names meant little or nothing to me, although the news of Ernest Gripp's retirement from the University of Iowa did make an impression, as did that of Elmore Stinchcomb's retreat to an unmapped tropical island. "He said he was going to play his flute and dance naked in the sun. I hope he's better at that than he was at teaching."

"I needed someone to talk to," Tyler was saying, without the help of a telephone. "Believe me, this is as big a surprise to me as it is to you. I'll only be here a couple of days. I can get a room at a motel if you want. Jeez, this place is a disaster area—it looks like the cats are keeping you, not the other way around. Don't you ever have any human company?"

After handing me his coat, he backed off slightly. "I guess it could be worse. I was half expecting to find Day-Glo posters of Jimi Hendrix and Janet Joplin. To your credit, this place doesn't look like 1968. But you wouldn't know it was 1986 either. Maybe some wall art would help, not that I'm any kind of expert."

I noticed there was more gray—and less hair—on his scalp. He wore bifocals in tortoiseshell frames, and his body wasn't so gangly. He was beginning to look like his father. This, too, could be seen in the clothes he wore, the conservative navy blue sweater, the pleated gray slacks.

"Rod, you really need a girlfriend . . . or maybe just a friend, period." He was sitting in my living room because he and Trudy were contemplating separation. I had never seen Tyler drink before, but he was opening his second can of Coors when he asked if I wanted to go to church in the morning.

"You don't really believe there's a giant Sunday-school-teacher-in-the-clouds taking attendance?" I asked.

"I don't know what I believe," he replied, before telling me he didn't think it could hurt going to church "just in case the Bible is correct."

"Then maybe you should bow to Mecca five times a day, or sacrifice sheep to Asshur. Just in case."

"The way I see it," Tyler said, "there must be a heaven. Where else would people like our mother go? And anyway, what's wrong with having a little faith in something?" He took a sip of his beer. "You know, Rod, you're more like Father than you'll ever admit. Stubborn. Unshakable in your conceits. Has it ever occurred to you, you might not always be right?"

The stubbornness argument I could accept. But if Tyler was accusing me of inheriting Benton Huxley's cynicism, he was wrong. If I appeared cynical from time to time, it was only because I, like nearly anyone with an IQ over sixty, could imagine a world much better than this one. I preferred to think of myself as one of humanity's heartbroken idealists, a realist by default. I kept these thoughts to myself, however. I could picture Tyler taunting me with "Oh, that angry young genius thing again. Isn't that getting a little old?"

"Tyler, I always thought you were the one with a lot in common with Father," I told him instead. "You agreed with him on every issue. You always took his side against me. Weren't you ready to enlist during the Vietnam War? I was surprised when you stayed in school."

"Maybe I've grown up some," he said. "There is such a thing as maturity, you know. I think a lot of my actions then were just wasted attempts to please the old man." Tyler paused, and I noticed his eyes had grown misty. He took another generous swig from his golden Coors can. "Did you ever get the feeling Dad didn't love us?"

"I certainly never got the feeling he was all that fond of me," I said. "I don't know, I always thought he liked you, Tyler."

"Well, I never got that feeling. I would have given anything for a pat on the back or a few words of approval. I tried so hard to please the old man, only to learn it was impossible. All I ever got was frightened and hurt."

He added, "You took the easy way—the smart way—to get his attention. You pissed him off, pissed all over his world. You made him notice you. You'll probably laugh at this, but I used to be jealous of you. When we were at home, I wanted to yell at Dad, tell him where to take his zooshit, just to prompt some kind of response. And later, when your book got famous, I would have killed for that attention."

After amazing me yet again by finishing his beer in a single, impressive gulp, Tyler told me of his wife's miscarriage and how he had hoped a child would save his marriage. "This all must sound pretty boring to you, but I really want a family. I want a chance to do things right, to make up for the warmth and trust we were never given. You've got your way of fighting the past. This is mine. I want children who will know me and, when I earn it, love me. I want sons who will take my hand and lead me into the worlds they create. I don't want kids who will be afraid to talk to me. I don't want a repeat of our family history."

The death of my cats brought the pain of the world down from its theoretical plane and into my Denver apartment as Wagner and Brahms took their places in the blind, destructive march of evolution.

When Brahms died, I bought two cat caskets at the nearest pet supply store—I swear that's what the wooden boxes were designed for, since they didn't seem to fit any other specifications—sadly knowing I would need both. I knew Wagner had also been sick for some time. His appearance was bad, his odor worse, and he slept nearly every hour of the day. Although I suspected I had waited much too long, I took Wagner to a vet for the second time in his life. My friend looked up at me with green, all-knowing eyes, as if to say he knew this was goodbye, as if he understood more than I ever could.

"Can you make him well, or at least make him not hurt so much?" I asked.

"This cat has advanced feline leukemia," the elderly veterinarian informed me as he poked at my friend's aching, rotting stomach. "From what you've told me, I'm certain that's what your other cat died from as well. I'm sorry but there's only one way to take away his pain."

And so I made the hardest decision of my life when I instructed the vet to silence Wagner's song.

Like Brahms before him, Wagner was buried in City Park, in an extremely private, after-closing-hours ceremony. Their adjoining, unmarked plots lay only yards outside the Denver Zoo fence, within roaring distance of Tiger Island. It was a spot I'd visit often.

A few months later, after learning I couldn't outwalk the persistent, stabbing pain of my loss, I followed evolution's cold, imperfect example—I moved on, letting new life take the place of old. I replaced my best friends with two tiny, befuddled kittens.

I named them Darwin and Freud.

CHAPTER 10

FENWICK IS SINGING in the shower: "Raindrops keep falling on my head . . ."

This is not my bed. No cats are begging for breakfast. I am not in my Denver apartment.

"Just like the guy whose legs are too big for his feet . . ."

Last night's empty pizza box jabs me in the neck as I roll onto my back, and I know there will be no escaping this time. Although I don't believe in fate, I recognize it when I see it. The box also reminds me that Fenwick and I share at least one small thing in common: we prefer good food over "fine" food, even when someone as used to being overcharged as Uncle Sam is picking up the tab. I'm sure he likes Whoppers and Chicken McNuggets, too.

A shower, shave, and three Diet Pepsis later, I am standing on the curb with Fenwick. A black hearse of a limousine crawls to a stop, escorted by twelve sedans, equally colorless, excepting the arrangement of flashing reds and blues on their light bars, the only bouquets in what promises to be an otherwise drab funeral procession.

Fenwick opens the rear door for me, and Ms. Foster, seated on the far side, invites me to take the center position. Fenwick slides in beside me.

"Are you ready for your briefing?" Foster asks as the car pulls away from the curb. She tugs at the hem of her skirt, a quiet signal to me and her fellow agents—sitting opposite us on a rear-facing bench separated from the driver's compartment by a sheet of soundproof glass—to stop examining her knees.

"You're to open our window of opportunity," she says. "You'll be our eyes—"

"And ears," a bespectacled chipmunk of an agent chatters, holding up a microphone in miniature, fastened to a tiny, dangling antenna. "This is absolutely necessary, although we're . . . sorry if we're *bugging* you." He snickers without opening his mouth wide enough to spill the assortment of acorns he's hiding. Only Fenwick chuckles along.

Fenwick and the Chipmunk undo the top buttons of my shirt. Foster, to my disappointment, offers no assistance to the fumbling pair, other than to instruct them, "The microphone will have to go on the outside of the armor. Otherwise we won't be able to pick up a word." Next she says, "It's small, as you can see, but you'll have to be careful to not draw attention to it."

The bulletproof vest was Fenwick's gift from earlier this morning. "What exactly are you planning?" I had demanded to know after he retrieved two of the constricting, gray-green undergarments from the hallway outside our door, along with a complimentary copy of *USA Today*. "If there are any plans for this game, your terrorist is making them," Fenwick said in an attempt to calm me. "These vests are only a precaution, in case things get out of hand. Besides, one of these won't make much difference against a bomb going off."

Now in the car, I tell Foster, "You've got to let me go in alone."

"That's fine with me," Fenwick interrupts. "I hadn't planned on dying today." Foster glares at her subordinate with a look that suggests she might revise his plans for him.

She takes a deep breath and continues. "Your agenda is as obvious as it is simple. You will try to talk the terrorist into coming out, to see if you can get her to give up. Of course, we'll be listening to every word, ready to give you whatever backup you need."

"Maybe you can play on her emotions, seeing that she's a woman and all," Fenwick suggests, placing his life in further jeopardy.

Our procession eases through the barricades, at first, anyway. For though the police officers respectfully part to let us pass, showing themselves to be every bit as accommodating as the waters of the Red Sea, the photographers and camera crews are not so cooperative. They lap against the limo's steel and glass, trying to pull us into a deadly undercurrent.

"Don't slow down," Foster orders the driver, using the white phone on a small black table in the compartment's center. "Run them over if you have to."

The limo jerks to a stop about twenty feet short of a final barricade, one I wasn't expecting. Soldiers are lying on their stomachs in camouflage uniforms, protected by a knee-high wall of sandbags, their automatic weapons trained on a target that is still surprisingly distant. A second contingent of FBI agents is waiting for us, each one vying to hold open Foster's door. There's only one person standing on the other side of our car, waiting for me to exit. He looks frail, old, harmless. But at least he's not crouched over like Foster's sycophants.

"Jesus Christ," I mutter.

"No, just your father," Fenwick corrects me. "I contacted him after you ran away. He couldn't help, needless to say, but he insisted on being here for the showdown. For moral support or something."

After Foster and Fenwick issue my final instructions, which are basically a repeat of everything they said in the car, my father puts his hand on my shoulder and says, "Be careful, son."

I'm ready to go in.

The Burger King is sandwiched between a nondescript office building and a closed-for-business drugstore, its windows sealed shut with cardboard and tape, its entrance padlocked.

I feel like I am watching a movie. These small details seem distant, unreal. My legs are working independently of my brain, moving me slowly, steadily forward. I know they are functioning completely on their own because my brain is frantically telling them to stop and reverse direction, like someone viewing the movie at home, shouting with detached superiority at the actor on his television screen, "Don't go in there, you moron." The edge of my Safeway bag is soft and damp with the sweat from my palm.

Now I am pushing open the Burger King's glass door, and I note that the restaurant is larger than the ones I've frequented in Denver. I see a second dining level at the top of two wide, short flights of stairs, and it is there that I glimpse the hostage families, huddled together on the floor, between tables of Formica and plastic, like immigrants refused admittance to their fabled New World, now waiting to be forcibly returned to their homelands, broken and robbed of their ideals.

Yet something is out of place here—the expressions on their faces, perhaps. Could it be they're more curious than frightened? Also—can this be what I am seeing?—almost all of the hostages, adults and children alike, are wearing cheap party hats of some sort.

I walk past the stairs, into the main area. And see no one. Forcing a "Hello," my voice falters. A solitary brown plastic tray sits atop a table, a letter-sized envelope centered upon it. I see my name, "HUXLEY," written in large, red letters.

I take a seat and open the envelope, remove a sheet of paper folded into thirds. "Declaration of Rededication," it reads at the top. I begin to scan it.

Whereas the schools remain segregated, women are treated as second-class citizens, and Rush Limbaugh is taken seriously, the time has come for action.

Whereas the military-industrial complex, like a cancer on the belly of our nation, only accelerates its growth. Whereas the great white silenced majority slumbers in apathy . . .

I knew it—Fenwick was wrong again. Aaron Hamilton Scott is somewhere in this building, ready to call in his debt. Worse still, I can tell he is watching me, studying me.

Whereas the name Rod Huxley once signified hope and societal change . . .

I stop reading. "Whoever you are, wherever you are, you could have saved me a great deal of anxiety by simply mailing this to my Denver address." I hear movement behind me. "I'm sure the patrons of this Burger King would have appreciated that, too," I continue. "You must know . . . Oh shit."

CHAPTER 11

I AM BEING TOLD to stand, not with words, but with cold, hard metal, digging into the back of my neck. "Relax, for Christ's sake," I mutter. "The gun is unnecessary. I'll do what you ask."

I am taken to the rear of the main dining area, near the counter with its four silent cash registers. A sign overhead reads, "Express Line. Burgers, Fries, Sodas Only." Slowly, I turn to face my thus far inhospitable host. Without speaking, I point to the small lump on my chest and silently mouth the word "Wired."

Sara Lynn Caine smiles, giving me my third major jolt of the morning.

She looks older. The few short strands of hair that protrude from her stocking cap are sprinkled with gray, and there are wrinkles under her eyes. I see dark patches beneath them as well, although I attribute these to her recent embrace of adventure over sleep. The gentleness I remember is gone, especially now that she's stopped smiling.

"I can't believe this," I say, covering my tiny microphone with the cup of my hand. "I would never have guessed, even knowing you were on the East Coast somewhere. Jesus, Sara, have you lost your mind?"

"Yes," she says sternly, if quietly, letting me know I have chosen my first words poorly, "I have lost my mind. I learned some time ago it was of no value in this society, so I deliberately misplaced it. I can't recall many times when it's been of use to me in the workplace, or in my personal life, for that matter. You never seemed to care one way or another about what I was thinking."

"If you believe that, then why did you bring me here?"

Instead of answering, Sara motions me to drop the bag, then deftly unbuttons my shirt. Before I have time to think, "I came all this way to get laid?" she retrieves the bug, tosses it to the floor, and squashes it, appropriately, with a bulky army surplus boot. Except for its crumpled antenna, its tiny, broken parts resemble nothing so much as ash that has fallen from a cigarette.

Ironically, however, now that the microphone has died, our first attempt at conversation follows suit. Sara's pale blue eyes are staring at me, studying me. They make me uncomfortable, make me forget so much time has passed since they last exerted that power over me.

"You'll have to excuse me," I say. "I haven't had more than three hours of sleep since this began."

"I'd kill for three hours," she replies, using what I hope is a figure of speech.

She paces a few steps and stretches her arms. "I realize that what I'm going to say will sound crazy. It probably *is* crazy—I'm in no position to know right now—but as long as you've come all this way, you may as well hear it. The reason you're here is that I had things I needed to say and no way to say them. So I decided to bring you back from the dead. I've been scanning the new publications lists at the bookstores for quite a few years now, and I knew you never came out of your self-induced coma."

"I don't understand."

"I want you to write something. I want you to write something for me and for everyone else who's been trampled underfoot. A *Cookbook for Justice,* if you will."

"You're right. You have lost your mind. I'm wearing a bulletproof vest, for God's sake. Or perhaps you haven't noticed you're not the only one dressed for the occasion. Now you're handing out homework assignments? What have you done with the real Sara?"

"The real Sara went crazy trying to hold on to her ideals while everyone around her threw theirs over the side like so much cumbersome ballast. The real Sara needed purpose and couldn't find any. If you want to bring her back, you need to help restore that sense of purpose. Don't look at me like that. I've thought this all out carefully. Thanks to me, you're more famous than you were the first time. That's the main reason I did all this. I don't have to see a newspaper to know I've made you a household name. I've given you an audience, and now you've got work to do. If you had read more than the first paragraph of my note, you'd know this."

She adds, "I'm sorry, Rod, but there's a new rule on the books this morning. I invented it and I'm enforcing it. You can't just quit. There's too much idiocy in this world. Too much injustice. I know. I've been dealing with it on a daily basis. We have to fight it, and the best way I could think of was to make you famous again and get you to transform this anger into words. Words that people will actually read."

"But there are plenty of people doing that right now," I say. "During the few times I've turned on my television in the morning, I haven't noticed any shortage of concerned advocates or saviors-for-hire, all of them trying to sell books with their photographs on the jacket."

"Yes, but there are millions of us who need a voice," she says. "We'll take every advocate we can get. And as I keep trying to explain, you won't be writing 'just another book.' I've sensationalized you. You'll have people reading *Cookbook for Justice* who never open anything but *People* magazine and *Readers' Digest*. You may even reach a few of the jerks who actually need to be reached, the ones who've forgotten about little things like decency and dignity. A single writer can shape opinions, and that's how change begins. Hermits, as you may have figured out, don't have that power."

Sara must have sensed my incredulity, perhaps in my unstoppable yawn or the emptiness of my stare.

"How about some lunch to wake us up?" she says. "You still like cheeseburgers, don't you?"

She instructs me to call for "John." I hear footsteps on the stairs. Burger King Assistant Manager J. Kronzek plods into sight on weathered brown shoes, trudging past us to the kitchen to prepare our sandwiches, one of which is actually a cheeseburger without the burger. With his head bowed and shoulders sagging, as if gravity is somehow more intense in the rear of the restaurant, John stares only at the counter and floor. Sara and I are silent as he finishes his assignment.

"This is for the vegetarian," he says meekly, pointing to the sandwich on his left as he places our order on a brown plastic tray. "Would you like fries with that?" he asks without sarcasm.

John, like the other hostages I glimpsed as I entered the restaurant, is wearing a cardboard party hat. I see now it's a die-cut crown, bright red and orange, designed around the Burger King logo. Stranger still, he's taped a napkin to his shirt. The name "Geraldo" is written on it in black magic marker.

I ask why.

"We've been practicing for our talk shows upstairs. It was his idea," he says, motioning to Sara. "He gave us a list of entertainment agents so that we'll be able to negotiate the best deals with the tabloids and phony news shows after this is over. Some of the others are really getting into it. I'm trying not to get too carried away myself, given my professional status and all. I'm an assistant manager, you know."

"Well, have a nice day," he says, again showing no trace of irony. With the same concentrated slowness, he slogs his way back to the restaurant's upper level.

"Did you know some animals scream when they're herded into the slaughterhouse?" Sara asks, after I return from the counter with my fries but before I'm able to ask her what exactly is going on here.

"No, but thanks for letting me enjoy my meal," I say. I see the most fundamental difference which still exists between us. Despite her assertions to the contrary, Sara's ideals are intact. Where I might have said, "This is a terrible world," Sara would have replied, "Only because we make it that way. It doesn't have to be."

And what of the other possible gulf now separating us? While I'm tempted to simply ask her, "So, are you insane?" I know such a question would be pointless. Crazy people don't tell you they're crazy, they tell you they're Moses or Spiderman. And if anything, Sara seems too coherent. Much of her speech is clearly rehearsed; it has that mechanical, high-school-thespian quality, as if she's still trying to convince herself of whatever logic it may be hiding. Of course, she probably had nothing better to do than practice her delivery during her lonely first nights as America's most wanted criminal.

In one important respect, at least, she is still very much the same Sara I knew back in Iowa City—the same Sara who walked into the Iowa City Post Office on B-Day as nonviolent accessory. She never backed away from saying what she believed in, and worse, she often acted upon those impulses. She remains, after all these years, a testament to the dangers of sincerity. The dangers of confusing words with reality.

"You need to be careful not to eat so fast," Sara cautions. "I've done some background reading on hostage crises. Our digestive systems slow down when we're under extreme stress."

"Then this should qualify," I say, wanting to add, "You've researched this? Are the schools out here offering extension courses in terrorism, or did you subscribe to one of those Time-Life book series?"

I take a deep breath, but the air I taste is musty and stale. It is secondhand air, and while it may have felt good when I first walked in, I'm now convinced that the air conditioner has been down for some time. It seems odd that the FBI hasn't shut off the electricity altogether. Or perhaps the harsh fluorescent lighting works to their advantage, since Sara probably has no means of turning it off at night. She's always in their sights. And the effect they most likely desire has clearly been achieved, for the feeling in here is one of tightness, of being boxed in, or worse, caged, like disposable lab animals awaiting the return of their torturer.

I make note of the few scattered souvenirs of vacations gone awry, historical relics of an unexpected siege and surrender. A child's miniature purse, its plastic exterior a pretty seashell pink, sits alone on a tabletop, as if stranded there by an impossibly high tide. Three shiny silver packets of freeze-dried Astronaut Food have been abandoned on another table, jettisoned like so much space junk, alongside a bag from the Air and Space Museum.

These relics help me to imagine the controlled commotion that must have prevailed here just prior to Sara's arrival. Wives are reprimanding husbands, husbands reproaching wives.

"Didn't I tell you that tour would last more than an hour?"

"Herbert, you know I don't like onions on my hamburger."

"Why couldn't your sister have told us it was hot here in October? I'm burning up in these sweatpants."

Everywhere, children are screaming and standing on chairs and hitting each other with scientifically accurate toy dinosaurs. A three-year-old girl, trained to be a consumer for most of those three years, is crying for "Mickey." She already feels like a hostage, kidnapped by her family on a vacation that should have concluded in Mickey World, that magical place she's seen on television commercials.

The bickering parents are anxious to finish their meals and guide their custom-fitted vans back to the safety of sub-urban motel parking lots. The streetlights have already come on outside, and while these hearty Midwesterners may have come to Washington expecting to be shot at by black men on drugs, they don't want to encourage that possibility by over-staying their tenuous welcome. Needless to say, they are taken aback by the appearance of a heavily armed Caucasian wear-ing an oddly out-of-season stocking cap.

"It's just a holdup," they comfort themselves with nervous whispers. "If we stay out of his way, we'll be all right." A few minutes later, however, once the situation has been clarified, the recriminations and arguments resume, albeit now in greatly hushed tones.

"Didn't I tell you we should have eaten at Wendy's? You never listen to me."

"You should have put some money in that meter. There's going to be a ticket on the van for sure when we get out of here—that's if they haven't towed the stupid thing away."

Although I'm not saying anything, Sara reminds me to speak quietly, so her "guests" won't pick up any clues about their captor's identity—and because "the CIA can reconstruct conversations from the vibrations in a pane of glass. I read that in the *Post*. With your bug out of commission, you can bet they're doing everything they can to eavesdrop on our little reunion here."

I ask if she shouldn't have given John some food to take back upstairs.

"They had a huge breakfast, I guarantee you," she says. "Croissan-wiches or something like that. Don't worry, they've eaten as well as anyone ever eats in one of these places. If anything, their debriefing sessions will include tips on dieting. I even let them use the bathrooms when they need to. What kind of terrorist do you think I am?"

"They are a noisy bunch," I note. "Not at all what I'd expect from a group of hostages."

"They want to be ready for the talk shows," Sara tells me again. "I've assured them they can expect some impressive offers once this is over."

"The modern American dream," I offer, "or would that be winning the lottery?"

"By the way, I prefer to call them guests," she says. "I think that's the term they would prefer as well."

Sara takes a french fry from our tray and continues. "There's so much I need to tell you. So much has happened since you knew me. I sent you a letter a long time ago, about my job in Boston. I don't know if you got it; I never heard back from you."

"You probably won't believe me," I say, "but I actually did try to call you then. I was told you were no longer employed there."

"Really? You tried to call me?" Sara seems genuinely amazed. "I can't believe it. So miracles do happen." She pokes at her sandwich bun with the soft, greasy fry. "Unfortunately, there was a reason you couldn't reach me. I was fired for telling the truth." Sara starts to tell me about her trials in the textbook publishing industry. She calls it a "tainted world of compromise and ambition."

"Do you think it might be wise to finish this conversation elsewhere?" I interrupt. "While I'm anxious to learn what it was that led you from Iowa City to this Burger King, I'm more curious to know if we will be permitted to exit alive. I've been assuming all along that you have a plan of escape."

The look in Sara's eyes suggests she'd rather continue her history, but she nods her head slowly and says, "I suppose you're right. We'll have plenty of time to discuss this later." When she unveils her strategy for leaving the Burger King, I make one small modification. I suggest we use a certain FBI agent to our advantage.

"They know you're a woman," I tell her. "I suspect you wanted them to assume otherwise. What I'm proposing is a little damage control. He's good. You'll see."

A uniformly blond-haired family of Minnesota Viking stock is recruited and sent out with the message "Huxley wants Special Agent Fenwick to come inside" scribbled on the back of a Burger King napkin. Needless to say, they're all wearing the cardboard crowns.

As they near the burlap fortress, they are grabbed by dozens of camouflaged arms pulling them to cover behind the sandbags. It's the last activity Sara and I see for some time, and after fifteen minutes, I wonder if it's possible the plan is being rejected. I keep these suspicions to myself, however, attribute them to nerves. After all, I can't imagine Foster letting her subordinate off so easily.

I catch myself yawning again. Yawning and thinking of ducks, of the Iowa River on an undemanding spring afternoon, of fish that momentarily forget their place in the great chain of being and burst from the water's glassy surface, attempting to fly. I'm trying to reconstruct Iowa City's geography. Did the footbridge behind the Student Union take me to Hatcher Auditorium, or was there another pedestrian bridge farther to the north? Perhaps I'm thinking of the sidewalks that bordered the Park Road viaduct?

I look at Sara's pensive face and remember our sole antiwar demonstration. Were we really shouting, "Draft the pigs" in heartfelt unison? My memory is clear, yet distant and cold, stripped of emotion. It seems borrowed, as if I'd picked it up from a movie or television show, and I'm reminded of something I once read in a DCC textbook—that the molecules in our bodies completely replace themselves every seven years or so. Maybe the Rod and Sara who participated in that rally have since been taken over by the most devious of impostors—us. And maybe my recollections are actually second- or even third-hand memories.

Sara coughs, and I realize I've been slipping into the first seductive half dreams of sleep. "The Muzak getting to you?" she whispers, making me notice the aural sedative that's being piped into this restaurant through tiny, round speakers in the cream-colored panel ceiling.

"Has it been there all this time?" I ask. "Or is the FBI just now unleashing their secret weapon?"

"I think that's what they call New Age music," Sara replies. "I came up with a better name for it, though, while I was sitting here last night: designer jazz. And yes, it's been playing the whole time we've been here."

Needless to say, Sara is correct. These soulless musical stylings do sound as if they were "designed." Designed and then custom-manufactured to complement the soothing, desert-at-sunset pastels in the wallpaper and floor tiles, or the decor-by-committee wall hangings. "I thought you enjoyed all kinds of music," I tease my hostess. "Didn't you once tell me, 'My favorite song is whatever one I'm listening to at the moment'?"

"And I think you're confusing me with sweet, selfless Sara again," she says flatly. "This stuff reminds me of using the bathroom at Winston-Bailey. It's not very conducive to staying awake."

As if in answer to her criticism, we hear a rattle, then a rumble, furiously swelling into an avalanche of sound. It does what the Burger King's corporate vice president in charge of

music programming should do with his collection of tapes—
it buries the Muzak. The french-fry skillets are shaking violently, as are the chains and padlocks that secure the back De-
liveries Only door.

If this is an earthquake—and I know that's not possible,
even while my senses tell me otherwise—its epicenter must
be located directly on the other side of the kitchen wall. The
noise has become nearly deafening in its intensity, despite its
inability to locate a single plate or cup that's not made out of
tremor-resistant Styrofoam or cardboard.

Sara is shouting directly into my ear. On her third try, I
grasp her message.

"I said, it's a tank!"

As suddenly as it began, the quake gives way to calm—or
what passes for it here. "I'm sure it's one of their smaller mod-
els—the alleys here aren't very wide," Sara explains. "They've
been driving them behind the restaurant every couple of hours.
I think they're doing it to keep me on edge, like I really need
their help. In fact, all they've succeeded in doing is helping
me to stay awake."

"Tanks certainly appear to be more effective than caffeine.
I thought the FBI knew you had a bomb. It seems to me
they'd be more considerate of your emotional state."

Sara reaches under her cap to scratch her scalp and, exactly as I'd been hoping she wouldn't, returns to the business
of my reclamation. "You know, I still don't understand how
you could have surrendered everything," she says. "I don't understand how you could have just stopped."

"And I still don't understand why you thought you had to
save me. I don't need saving."

"Nonsense," she says. "Everyone needs saving. But I think
you're missing my point. I'm not doing this for you; I'm doing it for me and all the others like me. Whatever hells you've
been living in, Rod, you created them. The rest of us never

had that choice. We were drafted into this bullshit. We need a way out, and this was the best I could come up with. If you end up coming with us, that's merely coincidence."

"But there is no way out," I caution her. "I thought there was once, but I realized it was an illusion. I saw that even before my book was published, and time has only reinforced that opinion." I tell her how I had long ago come to see *Cookbook* as the equivalent of a fifty-year-old tattoo on a seventy-year-old body, a sagging symbol of youthful defiance permanently branded on a flabby, misshapen arm.

"Then maybe you need another tattoo," Sara suggests, "one that will draw attention away from the first. This time, choose a design that truly represents you, one you might still be proud to wear in thirty years. Rod, you must care about something."

Before I can say, "That's not fair," I turn to see a small, chubby boy standing on the stairway. His dark hair has been shaved above his ears in identical arcs—whitewalls, Tyler and I used to call them, back when we had been similarly branded. An olive green jacket hangs open to frame a bulging T-shirt portraying a yellow cartoon character extending the middle of his three fingers in front of the U.S. Capitol. I put his age at four or five.

"I want to go home," the boy implores in a soft, high-pitched voice.

Sara starts to speak, but I intervene. "Tell your parents the terrorist does not wish to be harassed. Tell them he'll let everyone go soon—unless any of you bother him again!"

Sara pinches my arm and whispers, "Let him speak."

"My tummy hurts from eating too much cherry pies and hamburglars," the boy says. "I want to go home."

Still whispering, Sara has me instruct the boy to gather his family.

"Wave these napkins in the air as you cross the militarized zone," I caution them as they prepare to exit the restaurant.

"And tell them to send Fenwick without further delay. We don't need any more tummy aches."

"What do you say, Bobby?" the mother says, while squeezing the boy's soft, round shoulder with her one free hand. The other supports a shopping bag of Smithsonian souvenirs. Like her husband and son, she proudly wears the Burger King crown.

"Thank you for the hamburglars and pies and toys," the boy says. I notice he is clutching a miniature red Burger King bus as he speaks. "I had a good vacation. I liked this more better than the boring old rocks and stuff."

As they exit, the mother pokes her head back in the door and says, "I still can't believe I'm really going to meet her. My friends back home will just die when they see me on *Oprah*. They'll never believe it."

At last, they are gone.

"You have a real way with kids," Sara says. "Talk with them much?"

"I practiced on the way here, as a matter of fact," I say, but not without reminding her that she was the one who rearranged all the family vacation and field trip schedules. This is not what she wants to hear.

"There were no field trips," she says. "There were no bus tours for retired church organists. That's why I came here in the evening, so I'd be detaining as few guests as possible. But I will admit to choosing this particular restaurant because it attracts the most tourists. The other Burger Kings do more local business, and I figured that had I chosen one of them, there was a real chance the customers would be better armed than I was."

"What if I hadn't come?"

"I had faith," she replies. "I had to. Even after all these years, I knew you wouldn't turn down an invitation for lunch at Burger King." Her tone, at least, is gentler now, more friendly and familiar, maybe more forgiving. "And . . . I knew you visited Lazlo Roach in the hospital. It's something none of our so-called friends had the courage to do. You're really not as good as you think at running away from things."

"But how could you know that? Lazlo was unconscious. Practically dead."

"He heard every word you said, Rod. He told me your visits really contributed to his recovery." Sara places her palm on my thigh, and I feel a stirring I haven't known for years— at least not with the assistance of someone else's hand. I quickly cross my legs to conceal this involuntary reaction. But I don't want her to remove the hand.

Sara begins to say something else but is interrupted once more, this time by the activity outside. We move quickly to the front of the restaurant and see two soldiers standing. They clear a small break in the sandbag wall and again take cover. A lone FBI agent walks slowly, reluctantly, into view, his eyes focused only on the pavement in front of him.

"It's finally happening," Sara whispers. "Thank God."

Then suddenly, to everyone's apparent surprise—Fenwick's included—a second man appears.

"I can't believe this," I fairly shout. "He's going to ruin everything."

The Special Agent is shaking noticeably as he enters the Burger King. His nerves are exposed, plainly visible in a recently acquired facial tic, in rapidly blinking eyes. My father, in contrast, shows no signs of nervousness.

"Agent Fenwick, I presume," Sara says in a gravelly baritone that startles me as much as it does Fenwick. He tries to lift a trembling hand but seems unable to move it. My father is staring at Sara from only a few feet away. His expression tells me nothing.

"You were supposed to come alone," she barks at Fenwick. "Who the hell is this?"

"It's my newly spontaneous father," I interrupt as I yank him to the rear of the restaurant.

"What do you think you're doing?" I ask as quietly as I can manage.

"I wanted to see him," he calmly whispers.

"Excuse me?"

"I wanted to see Scott," he says. "I'm sorry, but I've wanted to meet him for twenty-five years, to see what he looks like, if nothing else. Don't you understand? He changed my life as much as he did yours. He freed me from DCC by making me feel like a genuine financial planner. His grandfather forged one of the world's great rubber dynasties; he owned half of South America at one time. Your friend is a very wealthy man. Don't worry, I didn't come all this way to complicate things. I won't say a word to the FBI. The secret of his identity is safe. And so are you, because you can use my knowledge as leverage if Scott is ultimately planning to harm you, although I can't imagine why he would. You could warn him that I know who he is."

"It's not who you think," I almost say, but catch myself. "Thanks, Father," I whisper instead, seeing no point in depriving him of the illusion. "That would be helpful."

When we return to the front of the Burger King, Fenwick is asking Sara, "Are the hostages all right?" His words are tentative, hesitant. His breathing is forced.

"As all right as any of us," Sara replies, still using the faux masculine voice. "Now listen carefully. I want a clear route of escape, and I'm taking Huxley as my guarantee of safe passage—along with my little bomb here." She lifts the briefcase cautiously; Fenwick stares as if hypnotized.

"Don't even think of fucking with me," Sara warns him. "I've packed enough explosives in here to easily take out a city block—along with a few careers at the FBI. You have much more to gain by letting me go. So here's what you're going to do for me. You'll remove the cops, but don't clear the city. I want downtown Washington to look like it's supposed to on Friday afternoon. One thing goes wrong . . . Kapow!" The Special Agent jumps back an inch, then takes a long, slow breath to regain the little composure he had.

"Fenwick, we're not dealing with some confused babe here," I volunteer, using language I know he'll understand. "This guy is dangerous. Give him what he wants." Then, as Sara pretends to be distracted, I whisper, "I can tell you who he is later." Fenwick's eyes open wide, no doubt envisioning a big, handsomely furnished office in the District—and the end of shit assignments like this one.

"It's done," he assures Sara. He picks up his black walkie-talkie and speaks. "We need to give him an out."

Foster's staticky voice betrays surprise. "Did you say *him*? Are you sure?"

"Afraid so," Fenwick replies, playing the role I'd expected of him. "Grandma Moses needed a shot of insulin. She was wrong. We're dealing with a man, all right."

Fenwick's words are greeted with silence. And more silence. If time is passing, it is doing so imperceptibly. I hear footsteps upstairs, a toilet flushing. Outside, clouds slip between the sun and the earth, casting a pall on the office buildings on the other side of K. Sara looks as nervous as Fenwick does, as nervous as I feel. But finally, Foster's compressed walkie-talkie voice inquires, "So what's the plan?"

Fenwick repeats Sara's instructions, word for word, right up to the "Kapow," and within seconds, those words become actions. The soldiers in the intersection show themselves. They stand to form a sandbag brigade, then heave the burlap sacks from man to man, clearing an exit wide enough for one car. Once the space is visible, they march from our sight in a highly organized fashion, with a precision and grace more suited to a parade than a retreat.

Next, a gray Ford van with panel sides and white government plates emerges through the gap. A National Guardsman practically falls from the vehicle and, without any respect for protocol, breaks into a panicky run.

Sara's huge stocking cap covers her eyebrows and ears. "Upstairs!" she shouts at Fenwick and my father, holding the briefcase above her head. Fenwick surprises me with his speed and dexterity at navigating two flights of stairs. My father, discerning no need for such hurry, lags behind, proceeding at his usual, carefully measured pace.

"You, get ready to move!" is the command I hear. It is delivered at gunpoint. "Now, out of the building!"

I am distracted by a movement high above us, by something fleeting and undefined. I look up to where the walls of glass make way for sky and see a sliver of metal glinting in the sun. As I turn my head to face Sara, I sense alarm in her eyes. She opens her mouth, but before she can speak, I am hit in the chest by a well-placed punch—or by a train, perhaps, invisible and, stranger still, absolutely silent.

I am lying on my back. A distant voice is shouting, "Hold fire! No one is to fire!" Sara is leaning over me; there seems to be a halo around her shadowed face. An angel in a stocking cap.

"Is this what it feels like to have a heart attack?" I hear myself trying to say.

"You've been shot," Sara whispers.

"That makes more sense." These words are not quite so difficult to form. "What happened to the bulletproof vest?"

"I think it saved your life," she says quietly. She lifts her briefcase into the air as she speaks, warning the not-so-sharp shooters that a lifeless arm cannot support something as deadly and volatile as a homemade bomb. She may also be doing it to warn my father and Fenwick to move back inside the Burger King.

She whispers, "It's time to end this game. I thought I had things under control. Everything in my plan was so carefully worked out, but I was wrong. They tried to kill us. One of those bastards tried to kill us, and now you're hurt. This wasn't supposed to happen. I screwed up. I'm sorry." She closes her eyes as if in silent prayer, then says, "This can't go on. Just give me one last minute before I surrender."

"No, I'm the one who needs that minute," I correct her. "Let me breathe for a few more seconds, return some oxygen to my brain. I may have a plan that will get us to the van. Just help me roll over, onto my hands and knees."

Now I am crawling, receiving little cooperation from my arms and legs, but getting better as I go. Sara is walking beside me, bending to grip the tail of my jacket as if it's a leash and I'm a dog being led home after an eventful escape. I'm almost there. Almost within reach of the Burger King door. And now, to my surprise and Sara's as well, my father and Fenwick are lifting me and carrying me inside.

They seat me on a plastic bench near the kitchen.

"You could let him go," Fenwick suggests to Sara. "There are others you could take in his place." He stops short of volunteering for that position, however.

"Thanks," I muster, "but I'll be all right." Then, "Fenwick, I need your help. Tell Foster no more shooting. I did not find that experience particularly enjoyable. Also, tell her we need caps."

"Pardon?"

"Stocking caps. Black stocking caps. Tell her we need three dozen."

My request is relayed by walkie-talkie. "I'm worried for the hostages," Fenwick helpfully adds. "That shooting cost us time and credibility."

Within minutes, another nervous FBI agent is crossing K. It's the Chipmunk, and he's bearing a bulging green garbage bag, stuffed, no doubt, with stocking caps.

"Fenwick, go upstairs and get the others. Tell them we need their cooperation. Before you bring them down here, ask them to remove their crowns and don these caps. They can keep the crowns as souvenirs, of course."

Fenwick performs this assignment promptly and efficiently, his nerves no longer a handicap.

When the hostages have gathered on the first floor, I place one of the remaining caps upon my head.

Fenwick, the Chipmunk, and my father do likewise.

Together, we exit the Burger King, a ragged platoon of battle-weary conscripts in black helmets, advancing as one upon the idling van. Shielded by the others, Sara and I open the doors and take our seats. Several of her guests are waving farewell. One even shouts, "Good luck!"

Sara places the van in drive. There is a tap on my window. It's Fenwick.

"You dropped this on the pavement before," he says, while lifting the Safeway bag that could send Aaron Hamilton Scott to a country-club prison. "I doubt there's anything in here of interest to me. You need your underwear more than I do."

CHAPTER 12

ON OUR ASSUMPTION that the vehicle is bugged, the van's radio is turned on full volume, with the dial set between two shrill, conflicting stations.

"Are you sure you're all right?" Sara quietly asks, leaning close to my ear. "I knew I was putting myself into danger. That didn't scare me—I mean, not like it should have. But the last thing I wanted to do was hurt someone else. Are you sure you're okay?"

Our van is cutting into heavy expressway traffic.

"I'm pretty sure we weren't tailed," Sara says, then glances up in the direction of a helicopter fleet. "Except, of course, for them. But we'll lose them soon enough."

The pavement is cracked and swollen in places, looking like something out of a *Life* magazine photo essay, circa 1969, of bombed-out village roads in Vietnam. Where there isn't a hole, there's a bump, and the van is badly in need of new shocks. "I think we're going to bottom out," I say, staring at one of the more pronounced craters. "Are you sure that brief-case is safe?"

"It should be." She reaches behind her seat to spring its latches, and the lid pops open. Ignoring my Jesus-Christ-we're-dead shudder, Sara retrieves a paisley shirt and dark blue pair of pants. I recognize the trousers at once, my first and only bell-bottoms, maybe the first bell-bottoms in Iowa.

"You left these at my apartment," she says quietly. "Please don't ask why I held onto them. The answer is, I simply did."

The comb and small container of Vitalis, however, have never belonged to me, nor have the pair of glasses with the lenses removed. But I understand what I'm supposed to do with them.

Half a minute later, I lean over to consult the inside rear-view mirror—and instead of myself see Benton Huxley at forty-eight. "They say it comes with growing older," I note. "But this has got to be the fastest anyone has ever turned into his father. Hell, these could be his glasses."

A green sign straddling the freeway reads, "North U.S. 395." Sara takes a right exit, then veers left into a long, six-lane tunnel illuminated by fluorescent strips of light. She lets up on the gas and tells me, "Now put on the pants; come on, hurry," while the midafternoon traffic shoots past us, its drivers unaware they're passing tomorrow's headline. "I'm glad you haven't gained any weight," she says. "That was one problem I considered."

I struggle to fasten the snap on the waistband.

"Well, not too much," she adds with a smile.

Following Sara's instructions, I stuff my old clothes into the Safeway bag with the Aaron Hamilton Scott letters. I'm still wearing my lucky bulletproof vest under the shirt, however.

"Now buckle up and hold on," she softly commands. I look up to see the tunnel's concrete wall only feet from my corner of the van. "Don't panic, we're only moving about ten miles per hour," I am assured, seconds, if that, before we collide.

There is a car, a sky-blue Saturn, waiting not more than twenty feet from where we hit the wall. A tall woman in sunglasses and a dark, simple overcoat stands beside it. A scarf hides the color of her hair. The woman says nothing as we stagger from the van.

"Hop in," Sara shouts, using her regular voice. The Saturn's engine is already running; its keys dangle from the ignition. The smell of new car wafts from its air-conditioning vents, competing with the nostalgic aroma (my father's bathroom, the Dubuque High locker room) of Vitalis. Sara turns off the air and, using the controls to her left, lowers the front windows.

"I don't believe in air-conditioning," she says.

"Your friend's not coming?"

"No" is all I am told.

We accelerate rapidly, and in the rearview mirror on my side of the car, I see a dark swarm of FBI sedans, too many to count, taking up every lane as they enter the tunnel. Now, at last, I understand why Sara's plan had all seemed too easy. It *had* been too easy. The government had never harbored any intentions of letting her escape, only of letting her think it was possible so that she would at least free her hostages (the ones worth saving, anyway), then take her briefcase bomb far from the White House, increasing the likelihood that the occupants of that building would risk its detonation.

How, I wonder, could Sara have considered our escape to be feasible in the presence of hundreds, if not thousands, of America's best-trained law enforcement agents—even after taking into account the ever important Fenwick factor?

As we make a sharp right into a one-lane tunnel exit, the sedans converge upon the abandoned van. I can't imagine what Sara's accomplice will tell the agents, or what contingency plans Sara could possibly have for us now.

I am suddenly blinded by a wave of sunlight but can make out the shapes of trees and pedestrians. When my vision finally becomes whole, I see young women and men, the ink barely dry on their college diplomas, hurrying to and from standardized government-gray buildings.

"Those are the Senate staffers," Sara explains, her tone irritatingly calm, as if we're not being tailed and I'm her tourist cousin just in from Epworth, Iowa, for the week. "Each senator has a good hundred of them, working solely to keep him or her in power. Welcome to my neighborhood."

We stop for a red light, facing a pair of Do Not Enter signs. Sara signals a left. I consult my rearview mirror. The black sedans are back, teeming as they surge from the tunnel's exit.

"We haven't lost them," I tell Sara. "The cars or the helicopters."

"Just stay calm," she says. "And keep looking forward."

"I'm sorry, but I've never been in a car chase before. Hell, Sara, excepting an FBI limo that might as well have been a bus, I haven't been in an automobile for probably seventeen years."

The UPS truck ahead of us takes an unannounced right into a parking lot, and suddenly, finally, Sara appears to be frightened. The sedans are quickly closing in on us—tightening the net, as Fenwick would probably say—and the car we're now following decelerates to let the convoy pass. But the FBI sedans are slowing, too.

"Shit," Sara mutters to herself, not so calmly. "What are the odds of this happening?"

I could say, "How about one in one?" but I'm puzzled by the look of genuine surprise on her face. She clearly was not expecting the FBI to single out our car. Moving her foot from the gas to the brake pedal, she gently slows the Saturn while pulling over to the right curb, next to the No Parking This Side signs.

Now the sedans are stopping to our left, no doubt alarming the other members of our blocked-in caravan. "Isn't that the terrorist and the revolutionary?" the drivers must be asking themselves. "The wife'll never believe me. I wish I had my video camera."

A contingent of armored vehicles appears from nowhere to provide reinforcements, starkly reminding us, in case Sara and I could possibly have forgotten, of the seriousness of our situation. Except for the neatly lettered words "District of Columbia Police Department" stenciled in white onto their cold, black shells, the vehicles have the appearance of mutant sci-fi cockroaches made gigantic by some Reaganesque nuclear catastrophe.

"I'll bet this is the first time those things have ever been hauled out," Sara says. "At least the budget committees in the police department won't be able to forget what I've done for them."

The doors of the sedans are bursting open. My bell-bottom pants are feeling tighter.

But my terror turns to astonishment (some of it, anyway) as the feds bolt from their cars, guns raised, only to surround the automobile directly in front of ours. It's a white Honda Civic—I recognize the make because my brother drove a similar car when he visited me in Denver.

"Surrender the briefcase and gun!" the agents are shouting at two head-shaped silhouettes from a distance of three feet at most. "Slowly step from the car!"

A distinguished-looking, silver-haired man is the first to oblige. After extending both arms to relinquish a briefcase, which is promptly snatched away, he and his trembling grand-daughter are persuaded at gunpoint to recline on the pavement. The glossy leather case is carried to a yellow, metal drum between two of the armored vehicles, then cautiously lowered into the container. Shovels are presented, and the briefcase is smothered with sand, followed by a blast of water from a hose attached to the nearest corner hydrant, ably commandeered by District police.

While we may be safe from whatever dangerous documents are concealed in the briefcase, the man and his grand-daughter are still very much in peril. Their bodies have taken on the properties of magnets, pulling the barrels of a dozen or so pistols and semiautomatic rifles downward in their direction.

"Let's ditch the car," I say, as soon as I am able to resume breathing. "Now. While they're distracted. It's not going to take them long to figure out the enormity of their mistake. We've still got the real briefcase to bluff with if we have to."

"Stay in the car," Sara commands, employing something between a shout and a whisper. "Stay in your seat." But it's too late. I've clumsily released the latch on my door, and it pops open ever so slightly. The sound it makes, to my ears at least, is equal in intensity to an explosion tearing apart a bulky metal canister and releasing a volcano of wet, heavy sand. It's the sound of defeat, the sound of "How the fuck can I be so stupid?"

One of the agents turns to face me. Two others do the same. Although their eyes are hidden behind matching pairs of black sunglasses, I know they are glaring at me.

The first moves closer and bends his head near our windshield. I see myself reflected in his glasses, and I'm startled by the disguise I'd forgotten I'd adopted. Christ, I do look like my father. The agent's gun is pointed upward, but I know this could change in an instant. He inspects my face as thoroughly as possible without actually climbing into the car and touching my features as a blind person might, then repeats Sara's instructions, made even more forceful by the volume he brings to each word: "Stay in your cars! This isn't a goddamn sideshow!"

The Honda is being dismantled, quickly and carelessly. An ashtray clunks across the pavement, only to be silenced by a thudding backseat cushion. Wisely (and incredibly, given what must be the temperature of the blacktop), the two suspects display no reaction, only lifeless inactivity.

Finally, an agent who has been silent up to now shouts, "Get these other cars out of here!" Two of his colleagues dart into the left lane to assume the duties of traffic cop. Slowly, one car at a time, beginning with ours, we are directed out of the net, through the few narrow holes between the FBI and District vehicles.

"This isn't your friend's car, is it?" I whisper as Sara steers our Saturn onto a narrow one-way street.

"No, she drives—"

"A white Honda. I'm sorry I panicked, but why didn't you tell me she gave that description to the FBI and police? Jesus, Sara, you thought of everything."

I turn to watch her smile in the daylight, and for the first time, I see her hair, free of the stocking cap. It's as short as I remember it but now mostly gray. The glasses are new as well, with their pale, plastic frames. I don't know when she slipped them on. But I'm relieved to see they complement her eyes.

Returning my attention to the rearview mirror, I observe a longer, hearse-sized sedan arriving on the scene. Foster is back, and I can imagine her look of astonishment when her door is opened for her. "So which one's supposed to be the terrorist—the elderly gentleman, here, or the girl?" Our luck, it is clear, may be short-lived.

"That was too close," Sara concedes as we cross a busy street named for the state of Massachusetts, aiming for a cluttered service station entrance. "I was leaving too much to chance. We need help. We need to bring my backup plan into play."

From the outer edge of the Conoco lot, where even before we arrive, twelve parked cars have been vying for space that is barely adequate for ten, I observe the orderly bustle of a Washington neighborhood. The main floors of row houses have been converted to restaurants whose sidewalks are lined with round tables and delicate white chairs, all tastefully arranged beneath umbrellas and sheltering trees. Despite the heat and humidity, which are every bit as oppressive as the day before, people are sitting and conversing in front of these restaurants. Others are walking or hailing cabs. A few lick the toppings from triple-dipped ice cream cones.

When Sara returns to the car, I ask her who it was that she phoned.

"Remember the Yappies?" she says as we cut back into traffic. "They held some kind of summit in Iowa City back when we were in the workshop there, before anyone knew who you were. That's who I called. You see, I read that the Yappies still get together every year. This fall they chose Washington, and even though there are only about eleven of them left, their choice of venue had something to do with the timing of your coming-out party."

"If I remember correctly," I say, "there were only about eleven of them to begin with."

"But remember how loud they were when they came dancing across the Pentacrest green?"

"Weren't they singing, 'We all live in a concentration camp' to the tune of 'Yellow Submarine'? You're right, it sounded like there were hundreds of them."

"I'm hoping they still live up to their name," Sara says.

"Weren't they the group calling for permanent retraining camps for everyone over thirty?"

"They've modified some of their views."

Before I can ask, "So what exactly did you tell the Yappies?" a black, four-door sedan cuts into the next intersection and stops. An FBI roadblock. As I expected, it didn't take Foster long to place her agents back on our trail. We are boxed in on all four sides, parked cars to our right, a yellow cab behind us, a silver Mercedes with white-and-blue diplomatic plates ahead.

A wine-red Plymouth Horizon idles to our left, its hatchback open to encourage the cooling flow of air when the car is in motion—and to accommodate two blaring stereo speakers as big as the ones I bought for my lodgings in 1972, when speaker housings were fashionably huge. Four teenage boys are listening to these speakers, which apparently blare whether the car is mobile or not. Their hair is shaved to the skin on the sides, a little thicker on top, where it supports the black-and-orange sports caps that match their jackets. They look harmless and young, barely old enough to drive, in fact, but their relentless, de-melodied music tells me otherwise.

They are gangsta rappers, looking for pussy to whip and whack, shooting at cops and shooting up crack.

"Don't stare," Sara says. "Keep looking forward."

Obeying her order, I notice that identical roadblocks are now in place in the other Massachusetts Avenue intersections. At almost precisely the same moment, three agents emerge from each sedan. Facing outward, they circle the cars with guns drawn to their chins, moving like dancers in a carefully rehearsed ballet conceived and choreographed for people and automobiles. Our three agents survey the traffic they've stopped. They shout at one another occasionally, point at specific vehicles. Twice, they point and stare at ours.

With little sense of rhythm, and even less regard for the sensitivities of his highly sensitized neighbors, the driver of the yellow cab expresses his displeasure by honking his horn—something he discovers he enjoys. One of the teens to our left requests that he "Cut that shi'," but it's too late. Cab drivers up and down Massachusetts have joined in a show of solidarity, leaving the cop-shooting pussy whackers no other option but to boost the volume of their speakers. *"Got me a rod and I got me a dick/The Man and the bitch, they both get the stick."*

I imagine Clifford Moss heading a record company, his office a lavish penthouse suite, the skyline of Manhattan glimmering, in the place of wall art, on all four sides. "The audience demographics for revolution may have changed," Moss enlightens the gangsta rappers newly signed to his label over expensive imported champagne, "but the marketing techniques have not. We act quickly, before the fad dries up."

Our three FBI agents, ignoring the cacophony, shout in unison and one points to a car on the opposite side of the intersection from us. They promptly surround the Civic on foot, their automatic pistols trained on its windows. "Surrender your weapons and briefcases and step from the car! Slowly, so we can see your movements!" Incredibly, these activities, too, are being duplicated in the other intersections. The drivers and passengers of two more white Hondas are being forced from their cars at gunpoint.

The District's armored fleet shows up exactly when Foster does. And though my view is somewhat obstructed, I'm fairly certain it's her limo I've sighted. It takes up both lanes of a narrow side street.

As an agent pulls open her door, Foster is greeted by a flotilla of gleaming white vans decorated with brightly colored insignias on their sliding side doors. The television crews are here. In an instant, dozens of casually dressed people are dashing into and through the acutely jammed traffic, each one holding either a camera or microphone.

"We need to get out of here," Sara gripes, almost imperceptibly. "What's taking the Yappies? They're losing their credibility with me."

"I'm curious to know how you were able to reach them in the first place. They can't be part of the 911 network."

"They're staying at the Sheraton in Arlington," she tells me. "According to the article I read, most of them are only part-time radicals these days. Most of the year, they work as insurance brokers, realtors, you name it. So though they still believe in sixties values, the Yappies don't sleep in public parks anymore when they hold their annual get-togethers."

Even as Sara says this, a caravan of dilapidated older vans is claiming the sidewalk—the only parking space left. But instead of the Yappie Convention of Sheraton Conference Room C, the protesters I met yesterday in Lafayette Park stumble forth from the vehicles' side doors. They must have followed the media here. And now everyone in the intersection is holding either a gun, camera, microphone, or sign.

"Stop UFO Secrecy," one of the latter is demanding. "Andromedans are people too."

"You realize we could still tennis-shoe it out of here," I remind Sara. "It would be as easy as stiffing that pizza dive in downtown Iowa City—the one with the very intoxicated manager whose primary reason for having a cash register was that it gave him something to lean on."

Sara starts to say something but stops herself. "Just stay calm," I'm sure it would have been. Suddenly, however, those words have become superfluous. Because for the first time today, there is reason to be calm. The guns are being lowered. The FBI agents are moving swiftly to their cars and speeding, at least to the extent that is possible, away. The helicopters follow in aerial pursuit.

The protesters and reporters as well are reclaiming their vans, then giving chase to the FBI.

Sara manages to grab the attention of a young journalist. "What's going on?" she inquires.

"There's a riot outside the FBI Building. Dozens of tourists are trapped inside, scared for their lives."

"They've had a rough week," I offer, before Sara cuts me off with a wounding sideways glance.

"Well, whatever," the journalist responds. "Someone in the building told us he could hear hundreds of rioters in the street, all of them singing about living in a concentration camp."

The Yappies have come to our rescue.

An older protester, his long, tangled hair painted a flaming sunset red, is the next to put his face in Sara's window. "You got any magic markers?" he asks.

I let Sara do the talking. "No, why?"

"We need new signs. The feds have shot and killed Huxley. Man, it's going to be like Chicago in '68 tonight." Finally, I knew what it took to mobilize a convention of middle-aged street fighters. A death. My death. The final ingredient in Sara's recipe for revolution.

"Don't worry," Sara assures me. "Plan B did not include an actual shooting. That was the FBI's contribution, and it was unnecessary."

Ever so gradually, Massachusetts Avenue begins to resemble a street again, as opposed to a Midwestern parking lot after a tornado. Only the cars that belonged here to begin with are left, along with a few scattered FBI agents and District police officers assigned to direct traffic. Fenwick and the Chipmunk, I notice, are manning the second intersection, with Fenwick standing in the center of our two lanes.

As we near Checkpoint Chipmunk, a scraggly, black schnauzer scampers into the crossroads. The car in front of us stops. We stop. The taxi cab behind us stops, mostly by using Sara's rear bumper as his brake. The driver hits his horn again, apparently the one skill required for licensing in this city. He moves his lips with an anger that sends seismic waves across his two chins, yelling something we are privileged not to hear. Slowly, excruciatingly perhaps, he extricates a nearly cab-size body from the vehicle.

"What the hell's your problem, lady?" he growls as he stomps toward Sara's side of the car. "I got places to get to. I'm running late."

Fenwick takes advantage of the standstill to examine the motorists gathered before him. Staring directly at us, he walks toward the Saturn, followed by the schnauzer. Fenwick's got that "I know you from somewhere" look on his face, but at the same time, I can tell he's looking for two males, at least one of whom is wearing a stocking cap.

"Look, if there's no damage—and I'm going to be gener-ous and take your word for it—I got places to get to, too," Sara says, mimicking the hairy, white globe of a driver. "Oth-erwise, I'd be glad to stay here and explain to you exactly how brake lights work."

The cabbie backs away. Fenwick loses concentration and bends to pet the dog, prompting Foster, still here, to our shared surprise, to shout from the sidewalk, "Fenwick, we've got work to do!"

It figures that Fenwick is a dog lover.

"We really should drive back downtown for old times' sake," Sara suggests, as Fenwick and the Chipmunk grow smaller in my mirror. "It's been a while since we've attended a full-blown riot."

"I've had my share of nostalgia for today," I say.

We turn right at a small neighborhood park onto another of Washington's narrow, one-way streets, where our already mugged-beaten-and-left-for-dead nerves are assaulted by a siren's sudden blast.

"Oh my God, it's just a car alarm," Sara exclaims. "A stu-pid, fucked-up car alarm warning its owner that someone is attempting to parallel park on his block. Like I said, welcome to my neighborhood."

Sara's third-floor apartment reminds me of my own, with its peek at the top of a capitol dome. There's even the faint scent of cat piss, a few evictions removed. This is the last of the similarities, however, because the room I'm facing is huge, cavernous—and like a cavern, it is mostly empty. A small black-and-white television is on in the distant corner. Not surpris-ingly, our story is the main feature.

"This is Helen Toxberry, live at the 395 tunnel." The en-trance behind her is blocked by dozens of police cars, FBI agents, and camera crews. Sirens are wailing and reporters are shouting. Helen is barely audible as she says, "I can't hear myself. This is fucking ridiculous. Why don't you run that tape of the victim again."

The woman I saw in the tunnel is sobbing now. "They stole my car, ran me off the road." Sara's accomplice describes a white Honda, a white Honda very much like the dozens, perhaps even hundreds, of white Hondas from which brief-case-wielding Washingtonians were forced today at gunpoint. Next, she is giving a description of me, in the clothes I had already removed in the van, and of a gravel-voiced man in a big stocking cap. "He had a bomb!" she squeals.

I wonder how she knew what I was wearing in the restaurant. But only for a moment, because the answer is right in front of me. The TV crews are everywhere—as they have been all day long—interviewing soldiers and cops, federal agents, and everyone who's ever worked or eaten in a Burger King. Hell, maybe they found some way to film me as I walked across K and into the restaurant.

"Do you keep your television on all the time?" I ask.

"Only when I'm not home," Sara says. "It makes burglars think someone's in the apartment. I never watch it when I'm here."

When I ask what there is for a burglar to steal, she replies, "How about my sense of privacy?"

"We'll have interviews with some of the hostages during our third half hour," an anchorman promises, and the television program moves to its next piece of entertainment.

"The riot outside the J. Edgar Hoover Building appears to be winding down. At least thirty people have been arrested in all, one for trying to make a Molotov cocktail out of a Perrier bottle. The president, speaking from his Camp David retreat, praised the FBI and ATF for having so many troops at the ready. He vowed to bring the terrorist to justice soon—before the coming elections. This promise may be based on recent poll findings, which suggest a majority of registered voters do not approve of terrorism. Here's the scene from earlier this afternoon, outside the J. Edgar Hoover Building."

We are treated to clips of balding, pudgy Yappies surrounded by hundreds of other protesters, all of them singing, "We all live in a concentration camp." Even the white supremacists have come to my defense.

"Another white male murdered by the Zionist Occupation Government," their signs now proclaim.

The segment closes with a shot that is destined to become famous, at least for a day or two.

"Hey, pigs, are you blind?" A middle-aged Yappie is pleading with police to arrest him. "I just burned an American flag!"

His tirade lasts a good thirty seconds, until one of the fascist thugs regretfully informs him, "I'm sorry, but your right to express dissatisfaction by burning flags is constitutionally guaranteed."

"Yeah? Well, what if I called you a motherfucker, motherfucker?"

"I don't see why you can't. Sure, go ahead."

"Man, this country's gone down the crapper," the Yappie grumbles, unknowingly paraphrasing my father from a long-ago speech that pretty much blamed me for the phenomenon. "The good old days are good and gone."

Next on the program, a conservative western senator is launching an attack on the FBI's "intrusive, unconstitutional practices." Just released on bail, the senator had apparently borrowed a staffer's car (the model and make of which he didn't need to mention) to ferry a fifteen-year-old prostitute to a drug bazaar in the Anacostia district before taking her home to his Virginia condo. Senator Crater, who, in the course of his up-until-a-few-hours-ago distinguished career, had proposed sexual normalcy tests for public-school teachers and mandatory church attendance for welfare recipients, burns red in the face with indignation. "We're talking a lifetime of public sacrifice and service," he sputters. "We're talking the reputation of a United States senator. Hell, we're talking about a $600 briefcase. What's wrong with these people?"

"Is that the guy in the white Honda we were following?" I ask Sara.

"Yes," she says. "The Honorable Eugene Crater, friend of the corporate logger and rancher. An organization I work with has been trying to bag that corrupt hypocrite for years. I can't believe I didn't recognize him. See, Rod, you've already accomplished something."

I could boast, "I'm sure you must mean, in addition to taking on the United States government and winning," but I realize the most difficult part of my personal hostage crisis—figuring out what I'm thinking, and worse, what I'm feeling—is only beginning. It's far too early for self-congratulations.

A helicopter flies low over the building, rattling the front windows. Sara asks if she shouldn't run out and grab us some food, "before I collapse for a couple of days into a well-deserved coma."

I ask if it's safe to go out.

"For me, yes. For you, no," she replies.

"Is there a Burger King around here?" I can't resist asking. "You know I've always liked their Whoppers. I hope your little escapade won't hurt their business."

"Ever the concerned revolutionary," she says, reaching to take my hand. "But I will say one thing now that this ordeal is nearly over. Their onion rings are good."

CHAPTER 13

DARWIN AND FREUD are on TV. My clever, beautiful cats, reduced to celebrity status. At least it's the *Sunday Evening News* and not *Inside Edition*. More importantly, I'm watching two healthy, energetic pets who don't seem all that traumatized by my disappearance from Apartment 503. There's even a hint of star quality as Darwin shamelessly savors this newfound attention. He's sliding around on his back while a woman rubs the white patch on his chest.

"He didn't tell us one of them likes to throw up," notes a narrow, boyish face with an out-of-season tan. "But we've got things under control here." The camera pulls back to reveal a carpet shampooer, the kind conscientious homeowners rent from Safeway and King Soopers. It's the size and shape of a vacuum cleaner, another appliance not indigenous to my apartment. Perhaps Freud will be thoughtful enough to vomit next on the kitchen counter, thereby persuading the FBI to give that room an overdue scrubbing.

The segment cuts to a reporter I recognize from one of the Denver stations, a stiff young woman with a chronic smile. She's standing outside, in front of the entrance to Arapahoe Towers. "These cats may be the real hostages in all of this. But we have some good news to report. Since News 4 broke this story two days ago, well-wishers from all over the Denver area have been donating food and toys—there is even one report of a kitty-cat trust fund being set up—to aid these courageous little felines, these small, furry heroes." I'm waiting for her to announce the informal viewer call-in poll. "Dial 432-PUSS if you believe cats are better equipped than dogs to handle a hostage situation, or 432-PUPS if you believe dogs . . . ," she pauses here for timing, "have the upper paw."

This is my second full day in Sara's apartment, although the first barely counted. That day, like much of this one, was lost in stage-four sleep, with me on the couch and Sara in a room I'd not been invited to enter. I can't recall even getting up to use her bathroom.

Earlier today—I don't know if it was morning or after-noon—I woke briefly to a phone that rang three times. Then, a couple of clicks and a hollow, tinny "This is Jack. Claire said you were due back at work tomorrow, so I know you've re-turned from wherever the hell it is you've been. If you're there, please pick up. And if you won't do that, then listen to me. I'm sorry. I'm an ass. Tiff and I are no longer together. I miss you. What else do I have to say?"

I wasn't so startled the second time. "Sara, this is Claire. I meant to call you Friday but didn't get the chance. I wanted to warn you that Plastic Man called the office again looking for you. I told him you'd be back on Monday. I hope that was okay."

Now Sara is cooking dinner: spaghetti with meatless sauce. She stands in the kitchen, in actuality only another segment of this great front room. Where the dividing wall should stand, the dingy olive green carpet—crusty in places, pocked where the furniture of others once rested—gives way to dingy gray linoleum. This is Sara's kitchen floor.

Sitting on her goldfish-orange, came-with-the-apartment couch, I am technically awake but don't feel completely present. Darwin and Freud are no longer fraternizing with strangers on network television; instead I'm watching a report on abor-tion clinic bombings. "It figures they don't consider this as newsworthy as the plight of your cats," Sara says.

When the spaghetti is gone, we forage for crackers, ched-
dar cheese, bagels, and frozen yogurt. Speech is not a priority.
I spill some egg-free mayonnaise onto my lap, and Sara dabs at
it with her napkin. Again, I'm forced to cross my legs. She
leans close for an extra few seconds, then pulls away slowly, as
if reluctantly.

"I have to work tomorrow," she says.

"I know."

Sara's not alert enough to ask how I would possess such
knowledge. "I've already used up my sick days on you," she
tells me. "Plus, I need to maintain a front on the off chance
the FBI has someone more perceptive than your friend han-
dling the investigation. You should be safe here."

I return to my couch, Sara to her refuge. The television is
off. For the first time, I notice how hard and lumpy the cushions supporting my back are. My discomfort isn't enough to
keep me awake, however.

The phone rings again in a room now dark save for three
stubby, translucent parallelograms cast on the ceiling above
Sara's front windows by a yellow-white streetlight. I hear the
click of her answering machine, but this time there's no message. Now I hear water running. Half awake at best, I rise
from my cushions and slouch toward its source. I open the
door to the bathroom and am bruised by a harsh, white light.
"Sara."

Without turning off the shower, she pulls back the clear
plastic curtain and throws her arms, followed quickly by her
legs, around me. With water splashing everywhere, we lum-
ber into the darkness I assume to be her bedroom, our mass
supported by only two legs, a *Kama Sutra* illustration come
awkwardly to life. I feel clothing under my feet, then wrap-
ping itself around my ankles. Conveniently, as if planned, we
fall onto a bed.

"Jesus, Rod, you're a wild man," Sara whispers, which sounds much better than the "clumsy man" I expected.

She stops to fumble with something on a bedside table, and the room, its ceiling and walls suddenly visible, expands and contracts. She's lighted a candle. In an instant, her body is on top of mine, pinning me down and stripping away the virginity I've reaccumulated over the past twenty years. My hands cup her moonlight-soft flesh with such firmness and need—such urgency and passion—it's clear they were designed for this and nothing else. I try to speak but issue something more on the order of a purr. I doubt Sara hears me. She's creating her own highly original sound effects.

When it's over—when my leg finally stops twitching and I'm no longer gasping for air—I say, "That was fantastic. It's like I've stepped into a place that exists outside of time, like this has always been here, just waiting for me to find my way back."

But Sara doesn't respond. Instead she gets up and hurries to the bathroom. "Go to sleep," she instructs me when she returns.

Unfortunately, I discover that sleep is not within my grasp. My eyes have adjusted to the grainy darkness; they want to stay open. I lie awake for what must be hours, my mind a brittle spider crawling slowly across the shadowed ceiling. I roll onto my side, watch Sara breathe and shudder, watch her breasts floating like lily pads beneath the thin white sheet.

"Are you still up?" she whispers at last, startled by my catlike vigil.

"Sorry, I thought you were sleeping."

"I'm trying," is all she says.

The following morning, Sara leaves early for work. There is no repeat shower.

"It's not safe for you outside," the note on the refrigerator reads. "Your photo will be everywhere. If you're followed back here, at least one of us will be going to prison. I'll see you at 5:30 or so. Until then, you're on the honor system.

"P.S. Please destroy this note."

There is nothing about the fire that passed between us. No "Can't wait to see you tonight" or mention of a "wild man." Something is terribly wrong here.

Compounding my frustration, this memo is the best her kitchen has to offer. There is no real food of any kind, only garlic and cucumber, four-bean soup, and something made from seaweed. Gone are the crackers and cheese—a less-than-satisfactory substitute to begin with for Little Caesar's two-for-$9.99 pepperoni pizzas—and the frozen yogurt carton looks as if it's been licked clean by a hungry Saint Bernard. Sara, it occurs to me, never really did like eating. Not like I do, anyway. How hard can it be for someone like her to go veggie? No wonder she's stayed so thin.

In a cupboard drawer, I find her pad of yellow Post-It notes. There's a pencil beside it. "We'll have to discuss my dietary needs," I write. This plea replaces the one she left while making her stealthy exit.

Halfway to the front windows, a question is answered for me: I *have* been looking at the same black metal desk she owned in Iowa City, now with even fewer bolts and nuts holding it together. Here's the dent where one of Red Vince's bottles had its flight cut short. And here on the writing surface, the "Free Bangla Desh" decal. On the floor near that desk, I see a small stack of books. These, I understand, are placed here for me. I kneel beside them and scan the titles of biographies. *Emma Goldman: Queen of the Anarchists* and *Return to Sender: The Trials of Margaret Anderson*. Other volumes record the struggles of Thomas Paine, Big Bill Haywood, and a few other "real revolutionaries."

I retreat to the kitchen, compose another note. "This isn't working. You need a new strategy."

But a few hours later, I am leafing through the first of Sara's suggested readings. Every twenty pages or so, a newspaper clipping reveals itself, and these, in turn, reveal their authors' concerns with every known species of injustice. All the usual victims are represented: blacks, women, Native Americans, gays. There's even an editorial designating English majors as an oppressed minority. "If you're too sensitive or honest in this society," the piece contends, "you're working with a serious handicap."

It's nearly seven when I hear footsteps in the stairwell. A lock turns and Sara blows into her kitchen like a gust of winter wind. Without asking, "How was your confinement?" she tosses me a small McDonalds bag. The burger and fries are cold, as is her practiced speech: "I'm sorry, but this is not what I was planning. Last night was a mistake. I'm not looking for a romance that will save my life. I'm looking for my life, period. I mean, I'm not ready for this, I don't think. It's simply not what I had in mind. It's not why I did all this. You're confusing me, Rod."

Cold and white—antiseptic—this room belongs in a hospital. Worse, it reminds me of the burn unit at the University of Iowa Medical Center, where patients are treated for bodywide bee stings. The tiles on the wall are as plain as the smooth plaster ceiling, as empty of color as the porcelain supporting my back.

Needless to say, Sara's bathroom merges seamlessly with the rest of her apartment. It's strictly functional, strictly fucking boring. She doesn't even use the back bedroom, save for storing a few well-traveled boxes, although its windows welcome the morning sun and an outside door swings open to a cozy balcony. And in the space she grudgingly occupies, there is no clutter, no record of life. Where are the old Leon Russell albums? The cat toys and speaker wires? This bathtub, at least, reminds me of my own. In addition to being adapted for showers by a landlord ideologically opposed to building and safety codes, it's a good half century old—and way too small. A stripe of rust connects the faucet and drain.

I am soaking the parts of me that fit because I cannot fall asleep. Tonight, the cushions on the couch are stuffed with twigs and gravel. Tonight, the words of Sara Caine are replaying in my head, and they're every bit as loud as the sirens outside. "I really am sorry," she'd said as I endured my limp, soggy fries. "I don't want to hurt you. But this isn't about sex. It's not really about you and me." By the time the eleven o'clock news came on, Sara had restated many of the points she'd made in the Burger King. And though she'd loosened up enough to laugh at my comment about the FBI's latest official statement, she concluded her speech with, "The one thing I didn't know when I planned this out was how I'd react to seeing you. I sure didn't think it would be this complicated."

After my bath, I stop in the kitchen for one last seaweed-and-cucumber snack and notice I'm leaving a trail of watery footprints. And this, like everything else I see, touch, and smell, reminds me of the night before.

Without the augmenting kitchen lights and the TV's tremulous glow, Sara's front room is poorly lit. The solitary white bulb is no match for this giant space; it burns like the sun, meaning that it's entirely adequate to those who live in the inner planetary circles but useless to the residents of Neptune or Pluto. This is why her desk faces the long north side, halfway between the kitchen and front wall. It's in the orbit of Venus.

The clock radio on top of that desk is predictably tuned to NPR—a suspicion I confirm by switching it on for a few seconds. In the big bottom drawer, now slightly ajar, I glimpse a stack of papers. With a vaguely forbidding rumble, the drawer rolls open. I know I shouldn't examine its contents, but then, I should be sleeping with Sara right now, so whose fault would this be? A press release serves as a cover for the pile: an in-house memorandum "RE: The proper recycling of in-house memorandums" is page one. Now I'm picking up a hand-printed note. It reads:

Sara,

I will be out of town for a week. While I'm away, please remove every trace of your life from <u>my</u> apartment. Except, of course, the VCR mostly paid for with my money. We are just too different. We want different things. Go save the world. Just leave me out of it.

Jack

Buried deeper in the pile, a second note:

Sara,

Where is the VCR? You had no right to it. Especially since it has my tape with the *GMA* appearance!!!

Jack

I also unearth what looks to be a draft of Sara's reply. Apart from the date in the upper right-hand corner, which reveals it to be eight months old, this is typed in the form of a single bulky paragraph.

Jack!!! You traitor. You hypocrite. I should have left months ago, back when your "evenings at the office" started turning into weekends. (That was when you first boasted your career was taking off. I asked then what I ask now. How can you possibly consider fighting for a worthy cause a career? Will your business cards read, "Jack Strickland, Vice President in Charge of Saving the Earth"?) I'd long known you were cheating on me. But that wasn't as bad as the realization that what you cared most about was seeing your name in larger and larger type. Finally, when *Good Morning America* called you about doing that spot on South American deforestation, it was like you'd been anticipating the call your entire life. You became the generic television talk show guest, as in one of those clowns whose only credential for being on TV is that they've been on TV. Your answers to Joan Lunden's questions were so flat and insincere, you could have been selling Pepsi-Cola. I've never witnessed such an instant transformation. New haircut, new suit . . . new personality. Pretty soon, there she was. The new girlfriend. And "new" is the key word here, Plastic Man. For Christ's sake, Jack, she looks like she's fifteen years old. You shallow bastard. All you ever wanted was a groupie. Someone who wouldn't remind you about sincerity and commitment in any form.

The letter-sized sheet is stapled to a receipt from the House of Ruth Women's Shelter: "Received, one Zenith VCR. Value for tax purposes, $150." A scribbled message traverses the bottom corner: "Ms. Caine, did you realize there was a tape in the video machine? Please stop by if you wish to keep it."

The sirens are louder now. Closer. Was that a gunshot? No, more likely a firecracker, or an older car rebelling. After all, what self-respecting thirteen-year-old fires a single bullet from a weapon capable of discharging four rounds per second? I stare at the papers on Sara's desk, which are not quite so organized as when I found them in their drawer. Is this where it began? Is this where she plotted her takeover of the Burger King, sitting in this chair, listening to the sounds of civilization shutting down for the night?

"Jesus, Rod! What are you doing?" Sara has a definite talent for sneaking up behind me. "Those papers are private. I really can't trust you. And the worst part of it is, after what happened last night, I don't think I can trust myself."

The hours pile up like the *Washington Post*s in Sara's "recycling stack," a homemade Washington Monument that occupies a corner in her hallway. By my estimation, this is the fourth-largest object in Sara's apartment, and it appears to be gaining on the desk and bathtub. I feel as if I've been here for weeks. It's only Friday. Day eight.

I've wakened each morning to perfect walking weather, yet I am permitted only to venture as far as the balcony, which overlooks a lush courtyard shared by the entire block of apartments and row houses. Washington's squirrels are still out in great numbers, leaping from branch to branch on the towering oaks or scampering across phone lines that converge onto a single pole. The most excitement I have comes with watching the red-haired woman on the third floor in the building directly behind Sara's take what seems to be her daily ten o'clock shower, straining my eyes as her tanned-out-of-season torso disappears behind the spreading steam, and watching my beard grow back.

I now know that the next time I hear Darwin singing in the night about an intelligent animal's right to face its own dangers and hunt its own food, I will better understand his song. For I will remember my own days of house-cat confinement, of being neutered and declawed, and worse, robbed of independent choice.

Unfortunately, I also know Sara is right. As she makes certain to remind me each evening, I'm a celebrity again, with my face on every front page and television news show. Even without my help, numerous Rod Huxley sightings have already been reported in all fifty states. Few commentators still believe I am dead, and nearly every terrorist group in the world is taking credit for planning "the Burger King offensive." (A handful, at least, are willing to share that curious honor by claiming I am part of their organizations.)

Sara, I have gradually come to understand, was counting on these developments. I have also come to appreciate something both Sara and Foster must have known from the beginning—that nabbing the terrorist early was critical to the FBI. The Bureau screwed up, leaving it now for either Sara or myself to do the same, and Sara doesn't seem willing to let that happen.

It's late afternoon now; I'm sitting on the black office chair, gazing with feline intensity out the front center window. The free peoples of Washington, squatty and machine-like from this angle, skim colorful brochures as they exit a basement travel agency, all the while balancing white paper cups from the Starbucks upstairs. The red brick church slightly off to my right is, according to my map, Capitol Hill Presbyterian. The smaller dome peeking out behind it must belong to the Library of Congress.

I am assaulted by a loud electronic buzz, a foghorn of a buzz. This, I gradually realize, is what my own intercom would sound like if it were hooked up—and if I had visitors. I look down at the street, and though I can't see the parking lane on this side, I'm fairly certain there are no idling UPS or Federal Express trucks nearby. Likewise for police cars and FBI sedans.

At last—with all due respect to the showering neighbor—something is happening. Something unpredictable. And this leads me to ask myself, "Sara, what have you done to me? First, you have me craving human company—and now, spontaneity?"

The intercom speaker is adjacent to the stairwell door. I push the button marked Listen.

"Ah hah! I heard a click. I know you're there. We really need to talk." It's the voice I heard on Sara's machine. Jack's voice.

Coming from somewhere in the back of my head, Sara's voice is telling me to keep my mouth shut and simply wait until Jack gives up and leaves. "The risk is too great. Find some other way to deal with your boredom." But she's not here to see if I obey.

Briefly I abandon my post by the intercom, letting Jack enjoy another of his clicks. He's still talking when I return. "I heard that, Sara. You can't hide forever. Why won't you talk to me?"

I place a dry dishcloth over the panel to muffle my voice. "This is the electrician . . . short in . . . -com. Miss Crane should . . . back soon." Sara, of course, won't be home for hours. I suspect that Jack tried calling her at work and was told by her friend that she was out for the day. "May I ask . . . name?"

He volunteers this information without hesitation.

"Mr. Ack. Could—"

"It's Jack. Jack Strickland."

"Oh, sorry, Mr. Ackland. Would you help . . . check the equipment? Only should . . . minute."

"Well, okay. As long as I'm already waiting."

"Could you speak while . . . connections? Do you . . . Lord's Prayer?"

This is easier than getting Freud to attack a crumpled-up piece of paper. Without so much as an "Are you serious?" Jack solemnly asks our Father to forgive us our trespasses and deliver us from temptation. "For thine is the kingdom, the power, and the glory forever. Amen."

The Pledge of Allegiance is not in his repertoire, however. "Sorry, I'm kind of a spokesperson for the environment and world harmony. I don't think I can validate any one particular nation. I hope you understand."

"That's too bad . . . almost got it fixed . . . something in the plastic. How about . . . song or two?" I'm trying to recall the titles of once popular songs with lyrics not likely to be mistaken for great poetry. "Do you know . . . 'Year 2525'?"

"You want me to sing?"

"No, just speak . . . plainly, slowly."

"'In the Year 2525,' huh? I used to love that song. It's strange you don't hear it anymore. But I don't know. I really don't think I can—"

Jack is joined by a second voice. "Excuse me, but who are you and what are you doing?" The woman asking this sounds as if she is far away, and I think she must be talking to him from inside the building, through the sash in the no–wackos–or–muggers–beyond–this–point door. "I know you don't live here."

"I'm helping the electrician. He's trying to—" She must have moved away from the door. "Sorry about that," he addresses me next. "I'm not so sure this is a good idea. Maybe we'd better stop."

"How about . . . 'Horse With No Name'?"

"Have you heard a single word I've been saying? I've got an image to protect. People in this town know who I am. I'm not going to—"

"I warned you." It's the neighbor again. "I'm calling 911."

"Put down your stupid cell phone and listen to me. I'm helping the electrician. He asked me to recite the Lord's Prayer and 'Horse With No Name.' Excuse me? Electrician, sir? Could you explain what we've been doing?"

I, of course, say nothing.

"Hello, up there. It's me. The guy who's been helping you."

Go, Jack, move. Before the police get here and start asking questions.

"Thanks a lot, jerkoff. I hope you never get that stupid intercom fixed."

"I'm warning you. I will press charges."

"Okay, I'm going already."

CHAPTER 14

"WE'VE GOT TO GET OUT OF HERE," Sara announces. "For both of us." It's Saturday morning, and she, like me, can feel the tension settling on the carpet and couch, the kitchen floor and the papers on her desk. "I know this might be stupid. But given everything that's happened this week, it's absolutely necessary. We can't stay locked up here all weekend."

Minutes later, Sara is steering her Saturn to Great Falls Park, past the infamous Beltway, north of the city. As one of the preconditions of my temporary release, I have been outfitted as a tourist. I wear a floppy, blue-striped hat with a badge that proclaims "I survived the Washington gridlock" and plastic yellow-framed sunglasses. But when I see the aptly named falls, with their turbulent, whitecapped waters and hissing, ferocious rapids, even I believe the disguise.

I am a tourist, and glad of it.

"So this is the Potomac's darker side," I say, standing on an observation platform, watching the waters cut sharply between slippery, knife-edged rocks. "This looks like something you might find in the Rocky Mountains. Or so I've been led to believe."

"I am absolutely amazed," Sara gasps. "I can't believe you've been living in Colorado all these years without ever once traveling into the mountains. Maybe you really are hopeless."

I am relieved to hear Sara laugh when she's finished, assuring me she does harbor some hope of redemption for me, however slight.

169

"So you want to know how to become a terrorist." Sara smiles coyly, now sitting on a rock wedged between two surging white jets of water and foam, well beyond the No Visitors Beyond This Point signs of Great Falls Park.

"No, I want to know how *you* became a terrorist," I tell her. "You don't exactly fit the FBI's profile, or anyone else's, I would venture to guess. As I said before, I certainly didn't expect to find you at the end of my journey."

"People have such stereotypes," she says with a devious laugh. "But it's all very simple, really. I tried to save the world and it didn't cooperate. I found that no one gave a shit—except me."

"I think you're leaving out a few details."

"I thought you weren't interested. At least that seemed to be true when I tried telling you in the Burger King."

"No, that wasn't true," I say. "I simply did not want it to be the last thing I ever heard. The FBI sharpshooters . . . the tanks . . . remember? If I weren't interested in what happened to you—in Boston and here—I wouldn't be asking."

"I think I did at least tell you I was fired for being too honest. Winston-Bailey, the company I worked for, had pioneered the art of producing inoffensive, information-free textbooks. Mostly, I went along with their censorship. At first, anyway. I did their dirty work by removing any and all substance from the books assigned to me."

"How do you mean?"

"Well, for example, in an introductory textbook on music appreciation, I cut all references to inner torment and social diversity. Beethoven was a cheerful, well-adjusted guy. There was no mention of his black ancestry or of the schizophrenia that ravaged his family. We even cured him of his deafness; in our book he suffered from 'audio impairment.' Wagner was apolitical, sort of a mischievous malcontent, and Tchaikovsky was no longer gay. In an anthology of American fiction, we had the slave owners in *Huckleberry Finn* talking about 'Afro-Americans.' I did attach a memo, at least, to those galleys, complaining we were making the villains look more enlightened than Twain had intended. I suggested we leave the original language intact, maybe add a brief prologue explaining its historical context. My boss, Dennis Dill, responded with a five-line memo of his own: 'In case you haven't heard, slavery's illegal now,' he wrote. 'Join the twentieth century. These books are not for the students, most of whom are just killing time. These books are for the PTAs and the school boards that set the budgets. Get with the program.'"

"So what did you do?"

"Like I said, I mostly went along with it. But after a few years of this crap, I finally devised my own moral solution. Whenever I felt it important enough, I would sneak my own edits past Dill's one-man censorship board. I became proficient at forging his initials. I was sure I'd never get caught because the empty suits upstairs never took the time to actually read any of the books they contracted. But I did get carried away at times. Like when I put one of your essays, 'Righting the Right-Wingers,' the way you originally wrote it, into a college-level anthology, *Radicalism and Resistance*."

Sara was only beginning to enjoy playing editor, she says, when a school board in Madison, Wisconsin, returned a large order of a textbook entitled *A World of History*. "It seems an atheist had objected to the mention of Judaism, Islam, and Christianity in a chapter about 'Middle Eastern Conflicts.' Heaven forbid. 'We're not in the business of printing Bibles,' Dill scolded me for the last time. 'You can pick up your final check in Personnel. And don't expect to find a job at any other publishing companies. You've destroyed a promising career. It's a shame. I could have taught you so much.'"

Sara starts to tell me what it's like to be blacklisted in Boston, to have rent due and not be able to secure even a job interview. But her tale is interrupted again, this time by a man in uniform, barking orders at us from between the trees onshore. It's a park police cop, telling us to move on, promptly.

"You should learn to pay attention to rules," he nips at our heels while herding us up a path to the official trail. Fittingly, he's wearing a brown shirt. "If I were in the mood to haul you in, you'd be in a lot more trouble than you'd ever imagine. I think you might really be surprised."

From inside his idling car, he watches us pull away.

"I can't believe this is the one time I get called for ignoring their signs." Sara grinds the gears of her stick shift as we withdraw from the lot. "Still, that was really stupid of me. Those park cops have a real inferiority complex. They don't get to use their guns enough or catch any real criminals. I read it in the paper. He could have brought all this to an unpleasant end. All we need is for someone to ask you for an ID, in any situation. I need to be more careful."

We're ten minutes into our drive before Sara is calm enough to resume my briefing. "I'd nearly resigned myself to a future back in Iowa when a friend showed me an ad for an editorial position here in Washington. Believe me, there have been plenty of times I've wished I'd never seen that ad." While passing a series of intriguing exits—CIA Headquarters, Bull Run, Chain Bridge—I hear why. When Sara talks about "phonies who traded their ideals for five minutes on *Good Morning America*," I keep myself from saying, "Jack, huh?" When she catches me yawning, I defend myself with, "Sorry. I'm not as young as I used to be."

"Rod, you were never as young as you used to be."

We've come to the end of a tree-lined parkway, and as we merge onto a wide, congested bridge, the gleaming white vista of Washington reveals itself before us. Sara is still speaking.

"I wanted to salvage something positive out of the wreckage. I tried writing something on my own, but while the words were full of passion, as you might guess, they weren't very, well . . . connected. There was something missing. Not that it mattered a whole lot, because I didn't have even the slightest chance of getting something into print. And if somehow, miraculously, I did get published, I knew no one would read what I had to say. No one. That's when I realized I needed help. So I kept pacing and thinking, and finally, on one of those late, late nights, I hit upon this, shall we say, adventurous idea."

"This was the hostage plan?"

"Yes," she says. "I started to feel strangely in control. In fact, once I realized I was actually going to go through with it, I approached the act with great care and planning. I read a few books. I stood in line for the FBI tour. I even called the State Department, posing as a reporter, to ask a few questions of their terrorism experts. Do you know why they didn't simply use some kind of gas on us in order to put everyone to sleep?"

"I hadn't given it much thought," I confess.

"Babies and children, that's why. The level required to 'take an adult down,' as the State Department calls it, could be toxic to a smaller person. 'Killing hostages is the terrorist's job, not ours,' I was told. Of course, that's what I wanted to avoid. I wanted to make sure none of my guests would get hurt."

"What about me?" I ask. "What about my potential injuries?"

"Try as you might to deny it, Rod, you were waiting for a wake-up call. You really do believe in everything I've been saying."

I think I recognize Sara's neighborhood. Yes, there's a street sign for Fourth Street, Southeast. My terrorist is silent now and in the best possible way: she's smiling like a stoned college freshman in a convenience-store snack aisle. I consider the possibilities for our evening ahead and am ready to smile myself. "Well, look at that," Sara says. "A parking spot directly in front of my building. This *has* been a good day." This is before she sees the man lurking by the door to the basement unit.

"Goddammit," she mutters, and I know the man's name.

Jack Strickland is coming toward us. He is, I can see, a reasonably handsome guy, his short, lacquered hair more blond than gray, his thinness making him appear taller than he actually stands. And now, to my genuine astonishment, I'm feeling a tightness in my stomach and lungs. Jealousy—straight out of a commercial for a somebody-gets-murdered, made-for-TV movie.

What Sara is feeling—and I need only glance at her face to be sure—is rage. Her eyes have frosted over, and this has the effect on me of February in Dubuque; it makes me want to bundle up and take shelter.

"Thanks again, Plastic Man," I curse silently. "I was really looking forward to sleeping on the couch tonight."

When I step onto the sidewalk, Jack's face is inches from mine. "Should I know you?" he asks. He's not so handsome at close range—the eyes are a washed-out gray, and not perfectly aligned. But I still feel threatened by his presence.

Sara cuts in quickly, "Tim, why don't you run upstairs and get dinner started. I'll join you in a second."

It's Monday evening now and Sara's home early.

"You've got to forgive me," the voice on the answering machine is pleading. "I didn't mean what I said. You surprised me when you showed up with that dorky—"

Sara pushes a button and the tape rewinds. Jack Strickland is silent. I can still feel his presence in the room, however.

"So have you written anything while I was at work?" Sara asks over take-out Chinese.

"Same as yesterday," I say.

"You wrote nothing yesterday."

"Then at least give me credit for finding my pace."

Sara's exaggerated groan makes it clear I'll be eating my garlic chicken cold, so I give her an explanation closer to the one she's seeking. "It is true that you've started me thinking about things I haven't thought about for a long, long time. About people I was certain I'd forgotten, emotions I thought were buried. Maybe these thoughts will lead somewhere. But for now, they are crowded and confused. They need to be sorted out. You need saving. The world needs saving. I need to take a long, cleansing walk. I need to see my cats. There's a lot more to coming back from the dead than I think you realize. I'm still convalescing. It's too early for me to promise anything."

I could easily add, "Thanks for the vacation. Let's do this again in twenty-two years. I'll pick up my own dinner on the way to Union Station." But there's something I can't deny: I am curious to see if my unexpected detour is actually leading me somewhere. I also can't deny I would like to double the number of times I've had sex in this decade. So I offer up something she probably wants to hear. "Don't give up on me, Sara. Not yet. I have been listening to everything you say."

Come the following evening, Sara is in a conciliatory mood, as evidenced by a chilled bottle of Mad Dog 20/20, "purchased for historical purposes." She smiles and says, "The guy at the liquor store asked me if I wanted a brown bag and a straw."

While we empty this vessel of syrupy nostalgia, Sara asks if I know what ever became of Rad Brad.

"The last I heard, he was working as a janitor in the Iowa City schools. He could still be there, but who knows? He could be anywhere. He could have fallen off the Earth."

We talk about others we knew in the days of hope and madness. Neither of us knows the whereabouts of Lonny or Carlos, however. "The good news," I note, "is that Red Vince never succeeded in taking over the world."

We talk about films we've seen in our respective neighborhood theaters and the books we've read. I tell her about Meg Reilly, Denver smog. The pleasures of feline companionship. I ask if she likes cats.

Sara tells me she does, but explains she's been too busy to keep pets of any kind. "But I've been too busy to do a lot of things," she says. "Until recently, I've been at the office a lot, preparing research for newsletters and press releases. You know, maintaining my front. Then, of course, all this came up."

The phone rings and Jack is back. "Come on, will you please pick up? Look, I don't know if that was an old boyfriend or a new one—he looked like an *old* one to me. I mean, Jeez, Sar', he could have been your uncle from Storm Lake. No one dresses like that in real life. But whatever, I will find out who he is. You can't shove me out of your life this easily. And, Tim, if you're listening to this message, go back to Dorksville, where you belong."

There's that damned jealousy again—even a fleeting urge to begin writing to impress Sara. Is she orchestrating all of this? Is Jack part of her plan? She can't be scripting his lines.

These are not the questions I ask, however. Instead, I say, "Will this Jack of yours figure out who I am? And if so, will he go to the police?"

"I can't answer the second half of that—he can be a real bastard when he wants to be. But I don't think he's smart enough to reach that point. You listened to his message, Rod. Only an uncle from Dorksville would fear Jack Strickland. I can handle him."

She yawns, smiles sheepishly. "Maybe we should try to get some sleep," she says. "See you in the morning."

By Thursday evening, Sara's no longer complaining about lugging my daily six-pack of Diet Pepsi up her building's steep, narrow stairwells—or about the corner store's rip-off prices. She's even purchased an inexpensive Walkman, along with a few cassettes, so I can listen to music. *Rubber Soul* and *Little Creatures.* Michelle Shocked and Rosanne Cash. And when she does lapse into her sermon-on-the-green mode, she at least tries to restrain herself. "You've probably forgotten just how much I helped you with your essays, making suggestions for revisions, telling you which ones I thought were the strongest. Remember? It seemed like nothing could stop us, and I loved that. We had hope. We had purpose. So tell me, why can't we go back? Who decided that? It's not like adulthood's been a resounding success for either of us."

Still, she refuses to say the words I am waiting to hear. Admittedly, I'm not exactly sure which words these would be, but they don't have to do with injustice or oppression, or any teeming, toiling masses. Only me and Sara.

I fall asleep to what sounds like rain, muffling the patterns of traffic and violence. Soon I will be dreaming, carried back to my Denver apartment, where I'll play with my cats, or just down the hall, to Sara's bedroom. Either way, I will wake up alone and disoriented.

Friday arrives and everything in the world is conspiring to piss me off. Sara purchased the wrong-sized batteries for the Walkman, and our red-haired showering neighbor, so punctual on other mornings, has chosen to stand me up. From the window below hers, a gold-and-white tabby is staring at me. He could be Freud, come to tell me what I already know: "This cannot continue. You must do what you've been contemplating. Tonight. Then return home and wait on us."

Back in the front room, I try numbing my brain with a television talk show, but the guests are so smug, sleazy, and just plain goofy, it only makes me angry. As Jenny Jones opens her mike to the third freshman Republican congressman who's seeking reelection, I turn off the set.

Now the clock radio reads 4:52. In just over an hour, I will confront my feelings about the woman who's become my terrorist—feelings that are gradually becoming less and less confused. More importantly, I will try to make Sara acknowledge her feelings for me. In preparation, while she makes her way home from work, I drink a glass of red wine from a bottle I found in a kitchen cabinet, surrounded by spices and cooking oils.

Even before I finish that drink, I realize it would be a good idea to have a second.

The Greek vegetarian pizza, I'm ready to concede, is quite delicious, although I'm having trouble eating and thinking simultaneously. Maybe I shouldn't have had that fourth glass of wine.

"My throat was very dry this morning," I still manage to say as planned. "I know it's from talking so much. I'd forgotten it could be so easy—or enjoyable."

Some time later, once Sara and I have rated the day's Rod Huxley rumors, I take my chance. "I've been thinking a lot about the past," I tell her. "Do you remember that night at the Coralville Reservoir? The night we named the stars?"

"That's the problem," she responds too quickly. "I remember *all* those nights. I remember watching your steady withdrawal—from me, from the world. And knowing it was intentional."

A fumbling for words, a change in approach. "But look at me, Sara. Look at me now. Can't you see how much I've changed? And that's only since I've been here. Imagine how much I could progress if you gave me, say, an entire month. Aren't you the one who gambled everything on the premise I could be salvaged?"

She parts her lips slightly, as if she's about to speak. But no sound escapes.

"Sara, have you listened to yourself these past two weeks? You say you want to go back to a time when life meant something. You say you want trust and honesty. But you're the one who fears these things. There's so much you aren't saying. So much you're afraid to acknowledge."

Nervously, she looks away, and I lean forward to kiss her— a move that works in Hollywood films but not Sara's apartment. She backs away quickly, stares at me with something between anger and confusion.

"I'm sorry," I say, "but you're not giving me a chance. What was wrong with our sleeping together? With our being together? Of all the things I've walked away from in my life, that would seem to be the one worth reclaiming. But look at us, Sara. You're turning this whole thing into a Three Stooges joke, a bad one, waking me up just to tell me I was sleeping. I don't understand. I can't understand. What do you want me to do? Go back in time and fix everything? Because as much as I hate to tell you this, it's fucking impossible. I can't prevent the bee-in by coming up with a better idea. I can't move with you to Boston instead of being a jerk."

I can't even think of what I should say next, so I tell her, "I need to get out of here."

I want Sara to beg me to stay, but instead, she only begs me not to leave—and this mainly through her same tired, "It's not safe for you out there."

"What have I got to risk? My imprisonment? I need to breathe, and there's no air in here. Don't worry, I won't mention your name if I'm recognized. I'm going."

In front of Sara's corner market, a man with frazzled blond hair is shouting slurred threats at everyone who passes without paying a toll. I am not excepted.

"Give me a dollar! Then screw you, brother, screw you. How would you like it if I followed you home, man? I bet your wife would like it, or maybe your dog." He looks like one of the Beach Boys, like the one who drowned, after he drowned. I try to ignore his madness, but the harder I try, the louder he becomes, so I duck inside a bar called the Tune Inn.

When my eyes adapt to the smoky darkness, I wonder how a Dubuque, Iowa, bar came to be located in Washington, D.C. Patsy Cline is on the jukebox, singing a baleful "Crazy," and the long, narrow room is packed well beyond any fire regulation limits. Stuffed animal heads, a modest preserve's worth, poke out from cluttered walls, as if their bodies are standing on scaffolding in the neighboring houses of business. "Belief is all you need to get into Heaven," a wooden plaque enlightens me. "You need cash to get a drink here."

In booths toward the rear, customers who apparently have that cash are ordering beer in pitchers wet with foam and condensation. A surly, older waitress snarls at me through the noise and smoke, instructing me to take an empty seat on a bench, to share one of the booths with two men and a woman who look like they were born about the time my book was published. One of them asks the waitress for a fourth empty mug so that I'll be able to drink from their pitcher. By way of thanks, I place a twenty on the table.

The young woman, I can't help but notice, is extremely beautiful—dangerously so, in fact—and it becomes obvious with time that her two companions both have crushes on her. They compete for her attention, listen thoughtfully to each of her comments. When she affectionately mentions "my senator," I first suspect I am drinking with the nefarious Senate staffers derided by Sara. But if anything, their conversation reminds me of a younger Sara Caine. Their words are so idealistic, so sincere. And in time, they have to do with me.

"I hear he's got a camp in the Rockies where he's been underground for twenty years," one of the young men says. "Timothy Leary's there, and so are Abbie Hoffman and Malcolm X."

"I thought they were all dead," his rival responds.

"Don't believe everything you read. I hear the hostage thing was something Huxley planned as a way to revive the Movement, you know, like a call to action. I hear he thinks the time is finally ripe for revolution."

"I read that all four Beatles were reuniting with the help of a psychic."

"No, that was the Doors."

"The sixties must have been so right on," the beautiful idealist remarks, her green eyes almost glowing, and I wonder where she lifted the terminology. Has Aaron Hamilton Scott been writing to everyone? "I'd really love to meet Huxley, to sit down with him face to face. I bet he could tell you what's really going down. He just seems to know, you know?"

Encouraged by my beer and the presence of what once would have been called mind-blowing beauty, I blurt my way into the conversation. "It was a wonderful time."

They all turn to face me.

"You're right," I continue. "It was a time when we expected things from life, demanded things from life." Even as I am saying these words, I can't believe I am doing so. Clearly, I have missed talking directly to others more than I had realized or admitted. The green eyes actually are glowing now, with a powdery luminescence, like that of the moon on a hazy summer night.

I order four shots of Southern Comfort, propose a toast "to stranger days," then savor the singe of holy burn on the back of my throat. "I knew a guy back in Iowa City, Rad

Brad, he used to call himself. He printed an underground paper. Everyone on campus read it, even the instructors. I used to write columns for him. It seemed as if nothing and no one could stop us, and it may have been true. Maybe we were the only ones who could have stopped ourselves."

After finishing off a second pitcher of Bud, my young friends suggest we leave the Tune Inn, inviting me to continue my storytelling "someplace cooler." Rather, she invites me along.

"Screw you and your grandmother," the maniac screams as we turn onto Fourth, walking away from Sara's apartment. "Come on, brother, give me a fucking dollar so I won't have to track you down and kill you."

On a dark stretch of sidewalk, outside of the streetlights' reach, a marijuana cigarette, its tip already burning, magically appears. When it is handed to me by a born-out-of-season-flower-child-goddess who's returning my gaze, I'm too embarrassed to admit I haven't even seen a joint since she was in grade school.

"We're going to Sheryl's place," one of the men tells me. "It's only a few blocks from here."

"You all right?" the other says, responding to an uncontrollable cough I've developed. "I should have warned you, this is pretty strong stuff. Don't shake your fillings loose."

But before we make it to Sheryl's place, just out of sight on a tree-lined side street, paranoia has taken over from coughing. I'm beginning to suspect that I'm walking into a trap. People aren't this innocent and trusting anymore, and Sara was probably right: everyone's looking for me, everyone knows who I am.

Instead of explaining my reasons, which aren't all that clear to begin with, I simply keep walking when they stop to share a final toke outside of Sheryl's row-house apartment.

"Hey, c'mon," she sweetly tempts me. "We want to hear your stories." I was right; it is a trap. I hasten my retreat.

"The party's just beginning. You can't leave now."

Swirling, blurring thoughts are shooting by like headlights in the darkness—the sensation of THC and alcohol surging through my veins, racing side by side without ever blending. I feel empty, even sick. Why couldn't I have gone to Sheryl's apartment? It was what I wanted to do. It was what she wanted. I know what Meg Reilly would say to me, were she to step from one of the passing buses or taxis, which wouldn't seem even slightly strange to me at this moment: "Why can't you just do things?"

And why can't I? I wasn't always like this. I used to act without thinking myself into paralysis. On a velvety summer night in Iowa City, Rad Brad and I wouldn't have turned down an invitation to a beautiful stranger's apartment. Quite the contrary, our hostess would have given up on getting us to leave long before we'd smoked all her hash and passed out on her hardwood floor.

So how did I get from there to here? Is this where I end up? Or is this the halfway point on a two-way trip, the lost on the way to found? I thought Sara was going to help me solve these mysteries, and this reminds me that as stoned and drunk as I am feeling, I am even more confused, because I've seen her eyes glowing, too, as brightly as those of any young Senate staffer. I've heard her laugh at the first jokes I've shared with anyone since I embraced hermithood, then look at me, quizzically, perhaps even longingly, trying to push away the years that hang like cigarette smoke in a Tune Inn bar, clouding our vision, burning our eyes.

"No, I don't know the way to the Washington Monument," I hear myself grumbling to some annoying, uninvited stranger. "Who are you, FBI?"

The beer, I think, is winning out over the pot. I feel the concrete buckling beneath my legs, but at least I've figured out where I am. The black, quivering shadows are those of the wide, round trees that stand between me and the Lincoln Memorial, now a shiny, perfect slab of marble, waiting to be sculpted. The concrete is a long, narrow beach, exactly symmetrical, and I am gazing, appropriately, at one of Washington's famous reflecting pools. Finally, I am throwing up in it.

CHAPTER 15

I AM REMEMBERING everything at once.

I am falling asleep in Washington, D.C., under a hazy, starless sky, but I am everywhere I've ever been. I am bobbing in an inner tube off the East Dubuque sandbar, an excitable, incitable sixteen-year-old momentarily subdued by something greater, held hostage by the Mississippi, its dark, concealing current as steady as time itself. I am pacing my Denver apartment, telling Oprah's "people" to leave me alone. "It's not my fault you've run out of guests. Unless you're planning a program on people who are acutely annoyed by talk shows and their representatives, please don't call again." I am petting a tiny kitten while Meg Reilly smiles. She seems as caring and open as the kitten on my lap. It's possible that I am smiling, too.

I am here, there, everywhere and nowhere. Omnipresent, but hardly omniscient. I am falling asleep in Washington, D.C., under a sky of orange and charcoal. Or maybe I'm just falling. Into and through the haze. Into the big city darkness that's never quite dark. Slipping from my inner tube, pulled beneath the muddy surface. A hostage of something greater.

Something is poking me in the stomach. Something hard and unwelcome. It's a nightstick, attached to a blurry, beefy District cop. My back is stiff, as solid and inflexible as the park bench beneath it. Vandals have caulked my sinuses shut, then cut out my tongue and replaced it with a dehydrated sponge.

"If you're alive, I think you should prove it by moving on," the cop says. The brightness of morning gives him an aura.

While picking the crust from the corners of my eyes, I request directions to Fourth and Pennsylvania, Southeast.

"They have a homeless shelter there?" he asks, before pointing the way with his battle-ready baton. "You just follow Constitution over there, up to where it turns into Pennsylvania."

Now I am walking uphill, up Capitol Hill, stopping occasionally to catch my breath and to read the tiny plaques on the trunks of trees—trees that, according to those plaques, have been imported from every region of the country.

As I near the actual Capitol Building, home to the government we were going to discard with such ease, I can't help but notice how exceedingly intact it appears to be. Clearly, it would take more than an underground hippie army—or even the near martyrdom of a thousand swollen Lazlo Roaches—to tear these walls to the ground. So how is it that not so long ago, the men who strut the halls of this building were giving oddly desperate speeches about people like me, calling for exile and imprisonment, for the banning and burning of books, as if we had stumbled upon some dark, frightening truth?

With the sun warming my face and causing me to shield my eyes with my hand, it doesn't seem even remotely possible. Could they really have been so frightened of us? Or were they merely annoyed by our insolence and brashness? Perhaps it was their way of telling us, "We'll teach you punks how to say, 'Fuck you.'" On this bright, reassuring morning, there is only one question: how could they have done anything but laugh at us?

In front of the Supreme Court Building (I've taken a minor detour), a young boy hands me a quarter. His mother, who only recently, it is evident, stopped relying upon those degrading elastic leashes, rebukes him harshly. "I told you, Billy, stay away from those people. They have AIDS."

The lunatic is already at it this morning, haranguing Sara's neighbors as they enter and leave the corner store. "I said, give me a fucking dollar, or I'll remove the gold from your teeth." Clearly, he works long hours. His job is more difficult than I first assumed.

Now I can see the front of Sara's building, and I'm hoping she's stayed home today, waiting for me to return. I'm anxious to tell her what happened last night—how I ran into someone we both knew two decades ago, someone who shares my name. I want to tell her, too, that Huxley appeared willing to renew the fight, or at least take part in an occasional skirmish, for *some* of the causes he once deemed worthy of sacrifice and risk.

Fourth Street seems strangely quiet this morning—until, that is, I pass the building next to Sara's. In the harshest of instants, I am mugged from behind, yanked from the gently massaging sunshine and the speech I'd been practicing for Sara by a wide, warm hand that covers my mouth. When the hand relaxes its grip, I am standing in the shadow of a black cast-iron staircase, in front of a door to a basement apartment. I turn to see a round, puffy face only partially obstructed by dark FBI sunglasses.

"Quiet, Huxley," the Chipmunk whispers. "There's a raid in progress."

"I'm getting tired of all these surprises," I tell him. "Or should I say, these onslaughts of abject terror. Please release me immediately. You're making me claustrophobic, paranoid, and more than a little irritable."

Except for motioning me to keep quiet, my newest captor ignores me. Finally, a walkie-talkie hisses excitedly. He retrieves it from under his dark blue windbreaker, and a voice announces, "It's over. Come on up."

"Not quite," the Chipmunk sputters in reply. "I've got someone you'll want to see. Yup, you've got it. We're on our way." As he pushes me up the stairs, the agent tells me what has happened. "Looks like we've nailed your terrorist. We've been on to her for some time. She was strictly amateur. There was no way she was going to get away with it—taking hostages and all, then acting like it was some big game. She had to be nuts. Whatever she had on you, whatever it was that made you come back this morning, it's done. 'Course, I'm sure you've got a lot of questions to answer before you even think of getting your life back."

Sara's few possessions are scattered about the room, more cruelly than randomly. Fenwick stands in its center, encircled by a colorful swirl of clothing. He's clearly in charge of the maneuver (he's the only one not wearing the blue jacket with a glaring white "FBI" on its back), but there is no look of victory on his face.

"She's gone, goddammit," he snaps by way of acknowledging our presence. "Not a goddamn trace. She didn't show up at work this morning, and she sure as hell isn't here."

I feel a wave of relief slowly returning the strength to my legs, but I share Fenwick's sense of defeat as well. So much for taking Sara into my arms and telling her she was right. So much for listening to her admit her honest feelings for me after I revealed my plans for the books she's going to edit.

Fenwick says something else, but I can't hear it. A helicopter is hovering so close it sounds like it's performing a drum solo on the roof, using its blades as sticks. The Special Agent takes one last walk around the apartment, as if it's possible his suspect will magically appear in one of the rooms, her arms submissively raised. He stops, stares absently at Sara's desk—with its open, now empty drawers—and the noise drops in volume. The copter is pulling back.

"We've got a lot to talk about," Fenwick says, turning to face me. "I can't afford to let you out of my sight this time. You're riding downtown with me." He leans forward to recover my Safeway bag, then hands it to me.

"Special Agent," comes the cry from Sara's back room, "you need to get back here quick."

The Chipmunk, it turns out, has discovered the showering neighbor. But no sooner are we on the balcony than Fenwick's walkie-talkie stutters to life, "Kcch, kcch. We've got a situation down here. Must be twenty veterans at the street entrance, and they want to see Huxley. They're all trying to squeeze into the front landing. Oh Christ, there's a guy in a wheelchair blocking the stairs. He's got no legs. This is getting hairy."

Once again, Sara Caine has enlisted the aid of unlikely allies. And even if she did use an unflagging hatred of radical author Rod Huxley to activate these vets, I'm encouraged to know she did have a plan for emergency escape. Of course, I'm not supposed to be here—I'm supposed to be with Sara. This scheme to tie up Fenwick and his associates was intended to help the both of us slip out together, and Sara can be none too happy with me this morning.

"How are we going to get out of here?" the Chipmunk is anxious to know.

Fenwick, unfortunately, is ready with an answer, and it's not one I want to hear. The chopper.

"What are you afraid of?" he asks as I balance on the railing, his hands wrapped firmly around my ankle. The red-haired woman is watching us now, her body concealed by a bright blue towel.

"Jesus, Fenwick! They've broken through the door and are headed up—"

Suddenly consumed with motivation, I'm making that tenuous first step from Sara's balcony railing to the bottom metal rung of a floppy, retractable ladder, an ascent made even more awkward by having to clutch a paper grocery bag.

"Don't worry," Fenwick yells up at me, "I'm right behind you." It feels like I'm fighting a Colorado windstorm. The fat gray chopper eclipses the sun. "At least now you can tell them you've put in your combat time. Welcome to the jungle."

These words carry more dignity than the ones he shouts when he's clinging to the helicopter's ladder. "Jesus Christ, come on. Let go of my fucking shoe! I was in Nam, too. Show some respect for a fellow vet. Aw, goddammit, what are you going to do with a shoe? Give me back my shoe!"

Deep in the Hoover Building's labyrinth, I am questioned relentlessly by Foster, Fenwick, and a handful of new Special Agents, all of them humorless. One particularly bland individual introduces himself as an expert on "hostage identification syndrome," and I am tempted to ask what he does during the twenty-year interims between assignments.

"Why didn't you leave when she was out of the apartment?"

"Why didn't you call us?"

"Were you poking her?"

Foster clears her throat conspicuously while glaring at her subordinate. It is something she does each time Fenwick asks this last question, and he is given plenty of opportunities to repeat it.

I tell them I was scared. I tell them I was trying to talk Sara into a peaceful surrender, to diminish any prospects of violence. I insist it was strictly a platonic terrorist-hostage relationship. When I ask about getting a lawyer, they reply, "Why? You're not under arrest."

"Can I at least be assured my cats are being fed?"

I am reminded I am here to answer questions, not to pose them.

Foster tells me her department has located the hijacked Honda in central Virginia. "That's one thing we haven't been able to figure out—why she drove there first. And we definitely cannot figure how that one car made it out of the city. Didn't you see any roadblocks?" This, of course, is good. They don't suspect the presence of our tunnel accomplice.

"Did she get her car back?" I ask.

"Did who get her car back?" Fenwick asks, already forgetting the no-questions-from-me rule. Then the ever reliable agent gives me the name I've been planning to commit to memory. "Oh, Karen Binder. She'll have it soon enough, I suppose, once we've concluded our search for evidence. Why? What's she to you?"

"I'm not sure I can explain it," I tell him. "But I feel an affinity for the others who were terrorized by Ms. Caine. I don't need to remind you we've all been through hell."

Hours pass; it must be evening.

"Why didn't you escape when she was at work?"

"Why didn't you pick up the phone and notify us?"

My stomach grumbles in protest.

Finally, I am presented with a new question. "What can you tell us about Jack?" Foster asks.

"London? Nicholson?"

"This Jack." The tape from Sara's answering machine is played on a small black recorder.

"Sara, Jack here. Listen carefully. I did something terrible just now. I called the FBI and told them about your 'boyfriend.' You know, it wasn't too hard to figure out who he was; maybe you shouldn't have forced me to read his stupid book that one time. But damn it to hell, Sara, I've learned I still have a conscience. Get out of there now. I'm sorry."

I'm angrier than I've been in years, and quite ready to tell my interrogators what little I know about their Plastic Man, especially since Foster has just announced that food is on the way. But an honest answer won't help Sara—or get me home any sooner. "I don't know." A clue is the best I can offer. "But he sounds familiar. Like someone I've seen on TV."

All through this long first day, Fenwick follows me into the men's room. He even paces in front of my stall the one time I need to sit.

During the second day, he waits by the sink, pretending to check his appearance in the mirror. Come Monday, he stands outside the room altogether.

That night, I am no longer caged in a holding cell shared only with a pizza box, my Safeway bag, and a tinted photograph of Marilyn Monroe that a previous guest had glued to the wall. Fenwick and I are back at Best Western Midtown, where he is talking and I am listening.

They're deliberately being kind to me now, trying to make me trust them, acting out a standard good cop–bad cop routine, but without bothering to change the cops. Maybe they're hoping the hostage identification syndrome will work for them, too. At least Fenwick apologizes on behalf of the United States government for my "unauthorized shooting."

"It looks like there were two people out there who remembered your book. But he wasn't one of our gunners—we only fire at hostage takers, not their hostages. Anyway, I'm supposed to tell you he's been kicked out of the ATF."

I do not try to escape.

I save that for the following morning.

"Fenwick, how long are you going to keep holding my dick whenever I go to the bathroom?" I ask as we leave the interrogation room. "Why don't you do something useful, like fetching us a couple of Diet Pepsis?"

My strategy works, exactly as I expected it would. Fenwick is duly offended as he bolts from my sight, and I am in and out of the men's room in a matter of seconds.

"Have you seen my tour group?" I ask as I near the lobby's security station. "I've been lost in here for hours. I just know I missed the bus to the NRA Building."

No one tries to stop me—or even questions my story. Hell, I'm almost expecting to hear, "Have a nice day, Mr. Huxley" from one of the guards. They do appear puzzled, however, when I add, "You haven't seen any Vietnam vets hanging around the entrance today, have you?"

From a pay phone outside a McDonalds, I call Ms. Foster's office and leave a message with her assistant. "Tell her I needed some fresh air. We'll talk later."

With the help of my First Visit map, I aim for the subway stop on the far side of Washington's newest tourist attraction, the Burger King at K and Vermont. The line of video-shooting vacationers extends beyond the front door.

I wonder if this isn't the day Montel Williams is doing his talk show from the restaurant.

My features are disguised again with the tourist-parody sunglasses and hat. These props had been stored in my Safeway bag since the trip to Great Falls, although the badge has since been replaced by one that reads, "Don't blame me, I didn't vote."

After claiming a seat near the rear of a subway car, which is surprisingly clean and quiet, I retrieve the plane ticket Sara taped to the bottom of my bag. She must have placed it there just before fleeing—an act that almost makes up for her lack of trust in not telling me about the ticket in the first place. Someone else's name, that of a Hank Edward Fielding, is printed on the four-part form. Mysteriously, too, Fielding is flying home to Omaha, but I think I've figured out how Sara would have explained this inconsistency to me.

"The FBI won't be looking for a D.C.-to-Omaha flight," I imagine her saying. "So you should be able to fly out of here without winding up on *Inside Edition*. As for what you'll tell the FBI, Omaha is where you broke free of your captors. You were stuck in the back of a van, tied up and blindfolded. Never knew if it was day or night."

This is where I would have asked, "So I'm turning myself in there?"

"The FBI has a big field office there. And you'll have your brother for moral support. I know from what you've told me that you think about him a lot. This will give you an excuse to spend some time with him. And I'm sure that once the agents grow tired of hearing your story, the two of you will figure out some way for you to get home." At this point, I want to believe Sara would have added, "I'll meet you later in Denver once everything has cooled down. You're going to need an editor for your new book."

The subway deposits me some distance from the airport's main terminal, but I welcome the opportunity to walk a few blocks, to feel the breeze—and humidity—one last time before settling for the sterile, recycled air of airports and airplanes. I pass a small, nearly empty parking lot before entering the terminal. A sign by the lot reads, "U.S. Congress and Supreme Court Members Only."

With some apprehension, I count the smaller children who scurry in the direction of my gate, often leaving far behind their useless, distracted parents. A travel poster encased in glass on a corridor wall comforts arriving passengers: "Eight million tourists visited Washington this year; only 27 were taken hostage."

One final obstacle is waiting for me at the check-in counter: I need a photo ID. "Let me get this straight. You have no identification of any kind." The airline representative, who's probably about my age but looks much older, studies me through sagging bloodhound eyes. "This is a very expensive open-ended ticket. I find it hard to believe you're traveling empty-handed. Is there anything you can show me ... or give me perhaps?" It takes me a second to understand what he's saying. But this time, the twenties come in handy. "Careful. Careful," he quietly scolds me. "You don't need to let everyone see."

Waiting for permission to board, I wonder what Sara would say were she here to wish me farewell. I know what I would tell her, beginning with, "Thanks for the wake-up call."

To my relief, my brother and his wife aren't interested in asking many annoying questions, and those they do put forth are along the lines of "Are you all right?" My brother even offers to drive me to Denver, agreeing that the FBI can survive one more day without knowing my whereabouts. He also bravely volunteers to make the call to Father.

"No, Dad, there's no need for you to be here," I hear Tyler saying. "Everything's under control."

"What's gotten into him?" Tyler asks me next. "All this spur-of-the-moment stuff. Did he really walk into the Burger King after you? I'm having trouble picturing that."

I meet their three-year-old daughter, Heather. She is, admittedly, cute, but the way Tyler and Trudy dote over her every fragmented sentence and uncoordinated action only makes me think of my cats. I want to be home.

"I see you're still getting all the attention," Tyler says, early into our long day's drive. "But there've been some changes in my life, too. It seems I did my job too well. Unions aren't so powerful anymore, and firms like the one I was with are no longer in such demand. So I ended up unemployed for a while, and it kind of made me think about the jobs I'd helped phase out for others, especially since I had a kid on the way." Tyler tells me he's working for an insurance company now, "a big one."

"People will always buy insurance, even in a depression," he says.

"I hate to sound like your big brother, but I do worry about you from time to time. I'm glad to see you're okay. You could call more often. I mean, I hope I won't have to wait for another hostage crisis to see you again."

Tyler amazes me with his performance in Denver, even if it is unnecessary. "It'll be fun," he assures me in the Arapahoe Towers stairwell. "You could use some privacy in order to decompress, and Lord knows I could use some excitement. When I tell the feds they've made a mistake, they'll have to let me go. Come on, Rod, from everything you've told me, it's not that hard to fool the FBI. Just call Trudy for me and tell her I'll be a little bit late getting home."

We push open the door to my apartment. Tyler enters. Three FBI agents interrupt their card game in my kitchen to ask him, "Who the hell are you?"

"Huxley," my brother replies, carefully saving his first name for later. "My name is Huxley."

The walkie-talkies are crackling again—"We're bringing him down right now"—and as I disappear around a corner in the Arapahoe Towers hallway, Tyler is led away.

The first thing I do when I get inside is give Darwin and Freud their favorite treat: a tablespoon each of Nutra Sweet butterscotch pudding with a little milk—fresh from the East Colfax 7-Eleven—on the side. It disappears quickly, instant pudding.

Ignoring me, they clean themselves, as meticulously as surgeons called to the operating room. When they are finished, I distribute the Washington souvenirs—the plastic Burger King straws sealed in slim white paper sleeves. The toys are immediately popular, or rather, one of them is, because Darwin wants the straw that Freud has selected.

A boxing match ensues, deceptively gentle at first, then escalating into a lunge-for-the-jugular jungle chase. Now I am completely forgotten as Darwin pursues Freud into the bedroom, where they crash, tangled hopelessly together, into the base of a lamp. The glass bulb explodes when it hits the wall. At last I am home.

After the cats have fallen asleep, one on the bed and one on the floor, I call the FBI's Washington headquarters. "I've told you everything I know," I insist. "But if you must harass me, you have my permission to send Fenwick here. Don't send anyone else, or I'll be giving my answers to the media."

"Just don't go anywhere," Ms. Foster says. "Promise me."

Fenwick arrives the following morning. "Jesus H. Christ. It smells like the Third World out there," he complains, referring, no doubt, to the permanent cross-cultural aroma of Mexican–Vietnamese–Middle Eastern cooking in the hallways of Arapahoe Towers. "It reminds me of Saigon. Ever think of moving?"

He takes a seat on my couch and accepts my offer of a Diet Pepsi, then instructs me to repeat the story of my abduction from the Burger King for what has to be the eightieth time, while he writes the information on a yellow legal pad.

"Slowly, slowly," he keeps imploring.

Next come the questions, the same ones I was asked in Washington. My answers are identical, too.

"I couldn't leave because I was frightened."

"I wanted Ms. Caine to be the one who called you, so that there would be no possibility of violence."

"No, I never 'poked' her."

In exchange for what he sees as my cooperation, Fenwick shares the following. "By the way, Huxley, you didn't exactly escape in Washington. This time, we really did let you go to see where you'd lead us. I mean, for Christ's sake, the questions were going nowhere. And it's not like we had a lot to hold you with." He fumbles in his briefcase, pulls out a small envelope. "Here," he says. "She mailed this to her address in D.C."

"Fenwick," the brief handwritten note inside begins, "Rod Huxley was an unwilling hostage. He stayed only out of fear. I am in this alone. But please tell Huxley he is not alone—he will be held accountable. Tell him we wait. Sincerely, Sara Caine."

"Where was it mailed from?" I ask.

"It had a District postmark," he says. "Not much help to us, of course. Not by the time we got it. She could be anywhere now. So what the hell did she mean about the 'waiting' stuff?"

"I don't know. But I'm glad to hear you deliberately let me go that last time. I'd like to believe there is some challenge in escaping you guys."

I do not show Fenwick the second brand-new letter, the one from Aaron Hamilton Scott III. The Special Agent doesn't need to know there are other would-be subversives out there, lurking at the drug orgies and cocktail parties of the rich.

"Right on, brother," Scott had typed. "It's great to see you're still shaking up the $ystem. Death to the oppressors. All glory to the BLA." There was no check attached.

"I guess we'll be seeing a lot of each other the next few weeks," Fenwick says as he leaves. "If you think of something you need to share with me, they've got me staying at the Days Inn in Aurora. Can you believe it? Shit assignments. They might as well make that part of my official title. Special Agent in Charge of Shit Assignments."

He stops outside my door.

"You know, Huxley, I'm getting way too old for this," he adds, almost as a postscript. "Do you think it ever ends?"

"I don't know," I say, "but I think I know how you're feeling. When I woke up in Washington on that morning you nabbed me, my bones ached. My muscles ached. Even my skin ached. But what hurt most was my brain. After years of willed senility, all the remembering was getting to me—that and sleeping on a park bench."

"Tell me something," Fenwick says. "Off the record. You were part of it all, weren't you, even at the Burger King? Don't worry, I'm not after your butt. You're like me, you don't start things. You just get dragged along. But what I want to know is how this Sara babe ever thought she'd get away with it. Didn't she ever think it seemed too easy? Can you tell me that?"

I feel reassured by what Fenwick says next. "We'll catch her, you know. It's only a matter of time." His words help me believe what I want to believe: that they have as much chance of apprehending Sara Caine as of catching the breeze.

Early this morning, after phoning my father to arrange a New Year's visit—and just before Fenwick dropped by—I purchased a copy of *USA Today,* and there I was, next to an article about a "superstar country singer" who was seeking a kidney transplant "so I can drink again."

Apparently, the FBI has decided to keep my reemergence a secret until they have captured their suspect: the all-caps headline above my dated photo blares, "Still Missing." America loves its hostages. No longer was I the "radical author," but rather a somewhat more heroic "generational writer" and "onetime baby-boomer spokesman."

But it was the last paragraph I found most interesting. "Clifford Moss, senior editor and vice president of Meiser & Grubb, yesterday announced an expanded, twenty-sixth-anniversary commemorative edition of Huxley's *Cookbook for Revolution.* 'This is a book for the ages,' Moss declared, 'but interest is peaking right now. Our philosophy at M & G is strike while it's hot.'"

As I have repeatedly told the FBI, I have no idea where Sara might be. She could be nearby, in that mythical retirement camp for sixties revolutionaries in the Rocky Mountains. Or she could be in another country. What I haven't told Fenwick is that I plan to hit the bookstores, as soon as it seems prudent, to learn what's left of the fabled Underground, to find out which enclaves, if any, have survived two decades of stifling, implosive change. I can only hope that wherever Sara has chosen to hide, books are published in English there. Then, at least, I will be able to keep up my half of the conversation.

Already I am working on an outline—something my *Cookbook* never had—for a preface and first chapter. And I have actually completed a dedication. "To the Breeze for stirring things up. And to the cats sharing my walk through this world: Darwin, Freud, Wagner, and Brahms. When I wake up in the morning, with my mouth dry and my sinuses pounding, trying to tear through my skin, and I'm dreading having to shower and shave, or even breathe, Freud hops on my chest and purrs, kneads the sheet with his paws, asks for nothing in return."

Once I have a few more paragraphs on paper, I plan to reward myself with an exploratory probe into the snow-crowned Rockies. What I will do is board the $10 shuttle bus to Central City's casino mall, then make myself AWOL and chart the banks of Clear Creek. Hike as opposed to walk, like a true Coloradoan. Sara, I know, would approve.

The cats are sleeping now. It's something they like to do. It's something I'll be doing soon, too, barring any new earth-shaking surprises. Darwin and Freud, at least, appear to be doing fine. I'm pleased to report that FBI Denver did a superb job of keeping their yellow water dishes filled and their litter box clean. In fact, I found a note from one of the agents asking if it would be all right to stop by and see the cats once in a while.

"I wanted to get some of my own, but it turns out the wife is allergic," he wrote. "I never would have known they could be so affectionate."

I guess that's what they got out of the deal.